HOLD MY HEART

HOLD MY HEART

KOJI A. DAE

GHOST ORCHID PRESS

Hold My Heart

PUBLISHER'S NOTE

As a work of adult horror, this book contains strong and potentially disturbing themes. A full list of content warnings is available at the end of the book.

CHAPTER ONE

Go in the south entrance of the West Tunnel. Take the first left. There will be partitions on the left side. Pass the first and wait for me behind the second.

Okay.

You're sure you want this?

Yeah, I'm sure. I'm ready.

———

The imbecile has no clue what she's asking for. Any kind of death is final, but the kind of brutality she dreamed up has a vastly different level of totality.

The distant sound of the boardwalk rushes in through my open window. The mix of laughter and screams soothes me and stirs the zhelani. But this time an unfamiliar urge rises from the creature. Not brutality and pain. Not even death.

1

This time, the zhelani wants something else and, though I can't name it, part of me knows it's more horrible than all the murders I've committed.

I stand and shut my window.

CHAPTER TWO

I pull my damp jacket closed as I duck into the gaping mouth of the West Tunnel. Waves lap the shore somewhere behind me, far enough away that they sound more like the white noise of a factory than the crashing glee of summer. Deep in the tunnel a roar approaches then recedes. Probably the subway, carrying a crowd of people to nightclubs and parties. The night is filled with destinations. Envy shoots through my chest and I take a deep breath of the stale air. For once, I have a destination, too.

A flickering lamp casts a yellowish strobe down the wide tunnel, dim and dirty and worse than pure darkness. I squint into the tunnel's depths, but anything beyond a few feet is a play in shadow and imagination.

It's almost 1:15. We agreed on 1:17—a specificity he insisted on.

You need to want this, he had written. *No mistakes. No blurry edges.*

Apparently he can measure the depth of my desire by my ability to shun round numbers.

I walk further into the tunnel, the rubber of my Keds

sucking against the wet concrete. Our meeting place isn't far from the entrance. I just have to take one turn down the first side tunnel and then slip behind the second concrete wall—specifics he sent in his last message, making me wonder how many times he's done this.

The agreed-upon alcove smells of stale piss and, strangely, french fries. My stomach betrays me with a rumble. I was too nervous to eat today, and the smell reminds me I will never eat again. Damn. I love french fries. The flickering light barely reaches here—there are pockets of full darkness in the corners. My sneakered toes fumble in a mess of fast-food wrappers, empty bottles, the occasional needle, and a used condom or two. Nothing I would allow myself to eat.

I pull out my phone to check the time. My numb fingers struggle to key in my pattern, and I'm not sure if my trembling is from the chill in the air or fear. The tunnels provide a pocket of warmth beneath the city—enough hot dampness that I let my cardigan hang open. So it must be fear. Who could blame me? The things I told him to do to me ...

I want to feel my chest ripped open. My flesh torn from me. My bones split wide. I want my heart to be held, still beating, as I die.

They were melodramatic, indulgent demands—things only a person who no longer cares would dare ask for—and I waited for him to refuse. Even then, I thought we were playing a game. There's no way I was talking to an actual serial killer.

He typed something. Deleted it. Typed something else. It took forever for those three dots to turn into words.

Bones aren't easy. It'll cost extra.

My hand goes reflexively to the front pocket of my too-tight jeans. Does he think it matters whether he charges two hundred or two thousand dollars? He could empty my bank account for all I care. It's not like I'll be around to spend the money.

My breath comes short, and I cough into my elbow.

1:16. In a minute, he'll be here. If it isn't some cruel joke. It's probably a joke. No one would do this for a living, and if they did, they wouldn't be hanging out on some chat room, offering their services to whoever wanders in. Except, there's been that uptick in murders. Women. Some older, some younger. A few men. One non-binary. All of them found with their stomachs split open and their guts spilled onto the floor, their mutilated bodies scattered around town enough to make it obvious this isn't a neighborhood thing. Ritualistic murders, the newspapers say. They were so depressed, desperate, unstable, their family members say.

What will they say about me?

Nothing.

There's no one to say anything.

I take a deep breath. Any second the clock will switch to 1:17.

My hand shakes, the light from my screen bouncing off the partition.

I can't do this.

I duck back into the tunnel, but a shadow covers the entrance, stretching along the dirty concrete. He's here. Right on time.

With a few skittering steps, I slip behind the first partition, pressing into the corner, out of the struggling flickers of light.

Footsteps splash in the small puddles. He reaches my partition and keeps going, as if confident he'll find me where he told me to wait. His silhouette is a head taller than me and his broad shoulders fill the tunnel. He hesitates as if he's a predator that can scent my fear, and that moment feels like a coin flip: as the coin lands I know what I want it to be, and I don't want it to be death.

My will to live rises as a squeak in my throat. The shadowy figure pauses, then walks on, keeping his head bent as he turns the corner where I should be.

I imagine him looking at the empty space, expecting me and not finding me. I should run. If I make it out ... what then? The West Tunnel is in the middle of the industrial district. Quiet at this time. No one to hear me scream. He assured me I would scream.

It will hurt. You will struggle. You will try to get away. I won't let you.

I had asked *and if I do?*

I'll chase you down.

My legs turn to jelly. I sink into the chill of the wall.

His head pokes around the corner. The light catches his eyes, turning them into slick oil spills that stare directly at my corner. He checks back around the partition, then edges towards me.

I press further into the wall, willing myself to disappear.

"Please." It's a hoarse whisper that tickles my throat and brings up a cough I struggle to swallow.

"Emma?" His voice is steady; not deep, but mellow.

As I nod my heart beats wildly, commanding me to flee. To survive.

"You're not where we agreed to meet." He has a certain charm to him, a dark gray overcoat cinching in around his waist, giving him an appearance of elegance even among the trash of the tunnels. "Is that on purpose?"

"Yes," I whisper.

He pulls back his hood, revealing short, shaggy hair. I squint to make out his face, but it's all varying depths of shadow. "It's okay. Consider our agreement cancelled."

"Cancelled?" I frown. "You're going to let me go?"

"It's a bother ..." He slips his hand beneath his coat and lets out a sharp hiss of air, then sucks in a deep breath as if he's trying to calm himself. "But you have to want it."

"But you're ... you ..."

"I'm a serial killer." He leans against the opposite wall, but his body is tense, his movements jerky.

I bite my lip and look away, as if he's said something embarrassingly dirty.

"It's okay, you can say it."

I don't look at him.

"No. Really. Say it." There's teasing in his voice, but a darkness rumbles beneath, like a storm on the horizon. *There's* the piece of him that I believed could hold a life and snuff it out.

My throat is painfully dry. "You're a serial killer."

He presses off the wall. It takes three long steps to close the distance, and then he's sharing my patch of darkness. I don't believe in auras, but I swear I can feel the vibrations of this man's body even an arm's length away. I want him to be attractive, because I imagined the man who would slaughter me having the chiseled jaw and broad shoulders of a movie star. Those are the only serial killers I've known until now.

I feel him assessing me, and I imagine what he's seeing. A short woman, overweight. Mousy shoulder-length hair that hasn't been washed in days and a nondescript face. I wonder if he's disappointed. But then, no. He's done this enough times that reality must have seeped into his expectations. How many victims does a serial killer have before the romance goes out of the act and it's just work?

"You intrigue me, Emma." It sounds like the pickup lines men use at the club when they don't realize I've already decided to fuck them, but there's something honest in the way he lets the words fall between us with no excuses or attempts to smooth them over.

"I intrigue you?" I stammer. My pounding heart slows.

"Yes. It doesn't take a brave person to plan their death. You could be brave. Or a coward. I could gut you and I'd never know. But it does require a certain bravery to stop a plan already put in motion." He looks down the darkness of the tunnel, then back at me. "This isn't the safest part of town. Let me escort you."

The irony of his words are not lost on me as he holds out a hand. It's slimmer than I expected, but steady. Waiting. Not demanding.

I hesitate. There's no way I can trust him. But what's the worst he will do? Kill me?

I slip my hand into his warm palm. He pulls me away from the wall, out of the tunnel, into the night where gray clouds cover the sky. Once outside, I don't dare look at him, as if not knowing his features can keep me safe.

He pulls me along at a fast clip. Puffs of silver breath bridge the space between us. A few minutes later the distorted music of the boardwalk drifts over our silence. I imagine people spinning on the tilt-a-whirl or rising above the city, waiting to be dropped on the double shot. The season must be ending soon, and it feels like those revelers have no right to exist so gleefully on a night like tonight.

He cuts away from the noise, into a residential area, and the decision of our motion catches up with me. I slow. The weight of me stops my would-be killer and he turns to face me. He's definitely not a movie star. His neck is skinny and his head seems almost too small for the bulk of his shoulders, but his shaggy hair and five o'clock stubble gives him a hint of ruggedness, and there's something attractive about that. A familiar primal urge swells in my lower belly. For months— years?—the only spark of life I've felt have been those moments of meeting at a club. Not sleeping with the random men, but that instant of eye contact. The thrill of possibility before the inevitability of action has been set in motion.

"How many have you ...?"

My question hangs between us. He squeezes my hand and yanks me towards him with such force that I collapse against his chest. His heart pulses steady beneath my damp cheek and for a moment I'm sixteen again and pressed against my first love in a summer storm. There's something fresh and new about him. Something eternal. When I look up, his face is sharp angles, thin lips and dark eyes, and I'm falling. Against him. Into him.

His lips cover my mouth. For how thin they looked, they feel full and soft as they spread mine apart. His arms wrap around me and I feel cocooned, his embrace spiderwebbing me to him.

Too soon, he backs half a step away, exposing my front to the cool air and giving him enough room to trace his fingers up the curve of my hip.

I stare at him. No more safety in anonymity. I set my jaw and challenge him to go further. He leans in. His breath is warm on my cheeks, and his voice is almost hesitant. "Come to my place."

"Are you going to kill me?" Teasing rises in my voice. This is a game I know, even if the script is new.

"If I was going to kill you, I would have done it back there." He tightens his grip on my hips and pulls me hard against him. My cunt responds with a warm tingle. "I would do it here and now."

I nod.

He leans in closer and whisper-demands, "Kiss me."

I kiss him, and he presses back hard, the sharpness of his teeth bruising my lips.

———

His third-floor apartment is disappointingly normal. It's not overly neat or clean. No signs of obsessiveness or pictures of mommy dearest. It's not sloppy with rotting food or corpses. It's the apartment of any late-twenties singleton. The only remotely adult piece of furniture is an immaculately polished, wooden buffet table near the kitchen. On top of it is a large, empty aquarium, as if he thought about growing up but couldn't even commit to stones and fake coral let alone the fish.

He scoops a bit of laundry off the couch so I can sit and pulls a bottle of whiskey from a cabinet. I shrug out of my cardigan as he pours two glasses without asking, and hands one to me.

"I don't drink," I say, waving the alcohol away. I hope he won't ask why. Discussing my current cocktail of pills is tiresome at best, and almost always a turn-off.

He shrugs, knocks one of the glasses back, pours the liquid from the second into the first, and sets it on the coffee table.

My eyes stay attached to him as he removes his dark gray coat to reveal faintly defined arms. Would those arms have been strong enough to pin me against the concrete and rip my beating heart from my chest?

As he turns, I notice a hump in his back, like muscles straining against his white t-shirt. But there's an unsettling asymmetry to them, and they almost seem to be undulating.

I rub my eyes and squint, but the movement is so subtle I can't be sure whether I see it or not.

He reaches into his discarded coat; pulls out a large, folded knife; and sets it next to the empty tank. The weight of the knife echoes through the apartment. The dark handle encasing the blade is maybe six or seven inches and has a strong curve, making the tucked blade wide in the middle and thin on each end. Hardly enough to split my ribs.

"That's pretty," I murmur, waving towards what might be the knife or the aquarium.

With his back still to me, he strokes the edge of the glass. The moment stretches out, and I wonder if I've said something wrong. The knife suddenly seems more capable as he picks it up and flicks it open.

"Come here," he commands.

"You said ..."

He turns and his eyes almost look tired. They're not the oily pools I imagined in the tunnel, but dark green, like the coolness of a forest. His cheeks are tight, his jaw clenched.

"I said come here," he nearly growls.

The command compels me. This is the strength that held him taut in the tunnels. It's the confidence I read on the message boards that made me think that I'd finally found a person willing to take action. I cross to him.

"I just need a little," he says with labored breath. His eyes are wide, white all around the irises, as if he's fighting what he's saying. What he's doing.

I fall back a step and furrow my brow, but before I can understand what he means, he snatches my left hand and runs the knife fast and hard across my wrist. I jerk away, but his grip is firm as he smears the blade with my bubbling blood. Once it's streaked with red, he releases me, and the tension in his shoulders melts.

Pain floods through me and I gasp, holding my wrist to my chest.

"Does it hurt?" he asks. His voice is softer. Sweeter.

"I ... yes," I stammer, trying to get control of my breathing.

"There's a rag on the counter." He turns back to the aquarium and places the knife next to it again, this time still open and dripping my blood onto the wood. I peer over his shoulder, pressing lightly against his back.

He whips around and grabs the rag from his kitchen

counter. I try not to think about what microbes might be in the fabric as he presses it to my wound. The searing pain eases to a throbbing.

I can't tear my gaze from the knife. It draws me closer, and as I lean towards it, I make out a faint droning. I can't hear it, not exactly, but I feel it in my chest—the buzz of voices singing a dissonant chord. The knife is more ornate than I first realized. The blade has strange swirls etched into it, and my blood seeps slowly into their crevices.

"What's—" My blood shows through the checkered towel, and I'm lightheaded. "I need to sit down."

His pressure is firm and consistent as he leads me back to the couch. My wrist throbs, and the spinning sensation doesn't leave my head. But instead of pain, I feel the beginnings of euphoria. I inhale deeply.

"So, where are the fish?" I say with a punch-drunk laugh.

"Fish?" He furrows his brows. "There are no fish."

Any sadness or exhaustion I thought I saw has left his eyes. He stares at me with an intensity I'm not sure what to do with, and the droning in my ears grows bigger, crushing against my body. My chest responds with an echoing buzz. His shoulders are definitely rippling now. Or else it's my eyes wiggling, the way they used to stutter when I was in my early twenties and taking whatever pills I could get my hands on for a moment of bliss. I lick my lips.

I want to ask what happens now, but my body knows what's next. He launches forward like a cat. His hands grab my hips and he's at my throat, grazing my neck with his sharp teeth, nibbling at my collarbone. He slows. Stops. His breath hits close on my skin, hot before the coolness of his inhale.

The rushing of blood fills my head and I swear the droning becomes a song—a dozen voices singing in the depths of a forest or perhaps the dampness of a cave.

Yes. A cave. This drone needs an echo.

I moan. "Please."

It's all he needs.

He flips my shirt over my head, revealing the expanse of my flesh. Red welts follow his fingernails across my dough-white stomach. My attention leaves the wound of my wrist and follows the new grooves of pain he draws on my skin.

I writhe beneath him, not to get away, but because I want him deeper. Reaching beneath my skin. The voices sing higher, a buzz of perfect harmony creating a vibration that turns my stomach and makes me giddy. My mind fills with images of this man ripping open my chest as I pull at the belt buckle pressing into my stomach. My skin's on fire and I'm opening to him, not just my legs and cunt, but every molecule. I sigh and melt into an expanse.

He covers my hand and firmly guides it above my head. Pinning both hands with one of his, he undoes the buttons of my jeans and slides his hand beneath my panties. A single finger splits my lips apart and I feel my wetness escape to cover the entirety of my sex.

I calm my twisting and wait. The droning voices have sank to a low grumble and my chest echoes with tiny waves.

He's slow and methodical—none of the frantic need I'm used to from my one-night-stands. He watches my face without shame as he enters me, one finger at first, easing himself in until he can pull at the butterflies in my stomach. And then two fingers. He makes a come hither motion, as if calling me out of myself.

"I am going to pull your soul out through your pussy," he whispers.

I'm not sure whether it's a threat or a promise, and I don't care. The droning has picked up again, a full chorus now, and I no longer hear what he's saying. My body tingles at the vibrations and I buck against his hand, driving him deeper into me. A wet pleasure seeps down my spine and I shudder with the first hint of a rolling orgasm that starts in my pussy and reaches through my stomach, making my nipples tingle and my throat open with a final moan of satisfaction.

He covers my moan with his mouth, his tongue forcing into my mouth, and something sweet and painfully salty drips along the muscle into my throat. I gag, but he presses harder against me. Finally I swallow, and he relents.

After, we lie on his couch, my head in the crook of his arm, his fingers playing idly with my tousled hair. I can't remember when I lost my clothes. He's still fully dressed, and I ache to unpeel him the way he has opened me.

"You came before we got to the good part," he says, tracing a hand down my still-tingling body.

I bite my lip. I want to say I can keep going, but something in him has shifted. The room is painfully quiet, and his playful smile does little to fill it. Even his body, which seemed to surround me moments ago, is less expansive. It's as if I came and he collapsed into himself. All I feel is the sharpness of his slender body where, moments ago, I swear there were muscles.

Suddenly, his eyes go wide, and he swallows what might be a burp.

"You okay?" I ask.

"You should go." There's that strain in his voice again. But more pressing, urgent.

"I ..."

"Go! Now!" he commands.

I get up and find my jeans and shirt cast off on the living room floor. I hop into the jeans in an awkward, jiggling, post-coital dance.

But he doesn't seem to notice. He's up and at the aquarium. He leans over and wretches into it.

My stomach roils at the black ooze that comes from his

mouth. It's just solid enough to be a continuous rope instead of spurts of liquid. My mouth drops open in disgust, and I grab my cardigan and slip out of the apartment while he's still retching.

In the hall, I jam my finger three times at the elevator button, then decide to take the stairs, before he finds me still here.

Outside, a breath of cool air hits my face and I put my cardigan on. I must have imagined those final moments. I bite my lip and wonder if I should call my psychiatrist for another appointment. It's been six months since I had my last appointment. Perhaps it's time to start up again. I take a deep breath and taste the salt on the breeze. A long walk home in the crisp air will do me good.

A smile flits on the corner of my mouth. The intensity of the night rests low in my stomach. It was unlike anything I've ever done, which is saying a lot. I don't have his number, but if he hasn't burned his account, I can still contact him. I want more, and I realize it's the first thing I've wanted in several years.

CHAPTER THREE

The woman is gone. That much is good.

I sit on the cold hardwood floor and watch the writhing black creature in the tank before me, trying to make sense of what happened. The zhelani knows better than to bring a victim to the apartment. We did that in our early years together, and we were always on the run. No sooner would I settle down than we would have to find a new city and go back to picking junkies off the street. I don't think either of us enjoyed those years. It's been decades since the zhelani has been this reckless. Unless it isn't recklessness. Perhaps the creature is bored with the city. Or cautious. There can only be so many ritual murders before cops start connecting dots. And if not the police, the local coven might get a whiff of the zhelani's power and start their chanting and spells to contain it. It's happened before, when the zhelani got so fat on sadism that others could sense its presence.

I haven't noticed anything, but I don't keep close tabs on the occult. Maybe this is the zhelani's way of telling me it's time to go since it refuses to communicate with me by any normal means. Still, this is ... well, I wouldn't call it sloppy only because everything about the zhelani is sloppy. It's wet and suckery with pops and wriggles. There's nothing neat about life with this creature, so the word sloppy holds no power. But careless? Perhaps. Or perhaps Emma was never meant to be a victim.

I shake those thoughts from my head and turn back to the tank. The zhelani is smaller than usual, filling only half the volume. It's withering away. Starving, in its own manner.

"I'm sorry," I say. Even after one hundred and ten years, I'm not sure if my parasite hears or understands me. "You know the rules. She has to want it."

The zhelani doesn't follow my rules, though. They are weak expectations I cling to in order to feel like I have any sort of say in our arrangement. In reality, the being exists and takes. It writhes and fills and eats. It doesn't censor itself. It doesn't wait. It doesn't obey. Yet here I am, denying the changes I've been seeing for the past year, and apologizing as if it can understand contrition.

My throat is raw from the passage of the creature. I can't call it vomiting. It's some sort of expelling, true, but instead of my stomach, my entire body feels empty, like the creature was wrung out of every cell of my being. I stand and the room sways around me. My head splits as if an axe has come down on it, and I lean on the buffet. It's an old piece, solid oak, purchased by my father as a centerpiece in our family home. It is the only thing I still have from that first life. Who knows how many times I have lost and found it again over the decades? It takes my weight, and I let the worst of the lightning bolt of pain pass before righting myself and picking up the curved knife, dark brown with the woman's dried blood.

My fingers vibrate as if a light pulse of electricity is running through the blade to my palm. Despite how empty I feel, the zhelani has still left part of itself in me, and I hate how comforting that is.

"Didn't get enough, eh? She was scared. I felt her heart pounding, her muscles weak ... that kind of fear used to be enough for you." I wipe the blade clean and close it into the worn antler. The woman was aroused, too. I can still feel the slickness of her on my fingers. And that's the part that frightens me: I remember the way she moaned.

I shouldn't be able to recall these details. But I remember the way the last one squirmed, her throat gasping beneath my palm as I—no, as the zhelani—squeezed. Her eyes opened in those final moments, a sort of instinctual relaxation beneath the pressure, the way fingers curl when a wrist is pressed. I remember her open eyes, so blank, staring right at me and seeing nothing.

"I shouldn't have to remember that." I slam my hands down on the buffet, the force echoing through my body. "That's our deal!"

My agitation causes me to vomit yet again. This time bile hits the hardwood floors. Just my innards—the last of the zhelani clings stubbornly to my wretch of a body. I'll have to clean up the mess, but for now I hold my aching head in my hands and kneel before the pile of sick, rocking back and forth, willing myself to not remember. I don't even miss the pleasure that once came after a sacrifice. I simply want the dark madness that relieves me from those memories. Because if they all come, the flesh I'll see and the screams I'll hear ... I bite my lip and clamp my eyes shut, closing all of myself to the recollections. Please. Let the madness come.

I stand and fling the window open, letting in an icy breeze and—there, in the distance—the scent of fried foods. Sweets baked in laughter. Corn popped in excitement. I lean half-naked out the window and let the sounds wash over me.

CHAPTER FOUR

Work on Monday is a worse hell than usual. It's hard to interpret the lines of code and SQL queries as more than busywork. They're a nice puzzle. Sometimes they're even a decent distraction. But never meaningful. I concentrate on the end product. At the moment I'm doing tweaks in our standard package that will allow our clients to sell LinkedIn profile pic modifications that are twenty percent more likely to get one of their customers an interview. Not a job, but a foot in the door, which is a lot these days. I'm not sure where their twenty percent claim comes from as we haven't even tested the software yet. But that's a problem for their marketing department.

I sigh and stretch and my screen goes blurry. I pick up the eyedrops and squeeze one salty tear into the corner of each eye.

"Rough weekend?" Monica asks from the next desk over.

"Huh?" I rub the liquid into my eyes.

"Hungover?"

"No, not exactly."

I'm struck with the urge to tell Monica what happened on

Saturday, but the details are as fuzzy as if I had gone on bender. I remember the messages and the planning and going into the tunnel—none of which I plan to share with my co-worker. I remember my heart pounding with expectation and fear. I even remember when the man showed up, his shadow stretching long in front of him. That much is clear. But after that, my memory collapses in on itself. The aching in my pussy tells me that we had sex, and the welts on my chest and stomach betray its intensity. I even have one deep wound on my wrist that is scabbing over, the crust breaking every time I change my position at the keyboard, letting a thin clear substance weep into my sweater. I'm sure the night was completely wild, but I can't recall the details.

And Sunday? It comes in flashes. I was in bed. Naked. Showering. It's like trying to remember a night on acid. Sensations. Moments. But nothing makes sense.

I pull my water bottle to my lips. A tart, medicinal sting coats my mouth, and I've been sucking down water all morning to wash it away.

"You met someone!" Monica says in a hushed exclamation that hints at more intimacy than we've built in the years we've shared an office.

"Maybe?" All I can say for sure is that I don't want to kill myself this morning, and I don't even want someone else to do it for me. Which most people would think is a step in the right direction. But it's not something I can admit to Monica.

It isn't that we're not friends. We've been going to lunch together for over a year, and occasionally we get drinks after work. Non-alcoholic beers for me and double margaritas for her. She's one of the few people who doesn't seem put out when I refuse to drink with her, and she's always ready to foot the bill for an Uber instead of using me as her designated driver. She's nice enough, and I know about her two cats and her fiancé even though I haven't met Jill. It's just that you can't tell someone at work about your death wish. There are some lines you can't cross. I can't even tell her about my usual escapades at nightclubs. The sex parties? Kink spaces? It would be too much. And yet, somehow, it's never enough.

"Let's get a coffee and you can tell me all about them," she says.

I look at my screen, the lines still blurred from the eyedrops. "Yeah, sure."

"You've got that look about you," Monica says as we cross the parking lot to the coffee shop. "Like, maybe this is meaningful."

"I've got that look about me like I haven't gotten any sleep," I counter. It's the walk of shame. A certain level of self-consciousness and guilt, even without the high heels and short skirt.

"Sure, that too," Monica says.

We drink our coffee and, despite Monica picking at my weekend like a dry scab, I don't give her much more than that I went home with someone, no I didn't stay the night, and no he's not "the one." Soon enough, our conversation drifts into its usual grooves. How're the cats? Jill? I'm happy enough to let the focus shift back to her.

But after the break, it's even more difficult to focus on work. I open one project, close it out, and go back to my tickets. Eventually I give in and boot up my personal laptop through its remote desktop so I can scroll through social media. It's not much better than work, though. One platform, then another, nothing holding my interest. I check Tinder for new matches, but none of the half-dressed men spouting variations on the same opening line pique my interest. *You're hot. Nice eyes. Love the cleavage.* It all boils down to: let's fuck.

I close out of it, leaving all of their messages on read, then stare at my browser tab. At this point, I've been dancing around my desire for almost an hour, and it's either open the code editor and get back to work or go to the site where I met my would-be murderer.

I know I shouldn't log into the site at work, even through the remote desktop. But I throw a glance over my shoulder and, safe enough for the moment, open my Tor client.

Getting the site address had been a slow process—first to learn what it was I actually wanted, then to find that it actually existed, and finally to get someone to trust me enough to give me the address. It took months of weeding through snuff sites, seeing videos that couldn't be unimagined once they'd burned themselves onto my consciousness, and chatting with handles like "deathgod2000" that mostly turned out to be angsty teens who usually suggested I get help when the truth came out. Nothing more humiliating than a teen troll showing concern for me.

Still, I kept on, and eventually I found DeathByRequest.

When I open the chatroom and click on his name, I find my private chat with DeathByRequest has been scrubbed. I hadn't chatted with him very long, but there'd been a few nights we'd typed back and forth until the sun shone through my living room window. Those were the nights I spent imagining what he would look like—always gorgeous in a way I couldn't quite force to take shape in my mind—and how it would feel to have his hands tearing the life from me. I spent the long pauses waiting for his carefully worded questions masturbating, coming multiple times throughout the night. But looking through those conversations probably wouldn't turn me on now. The words contained nothing significant. It was the anticipation of the actual act.

I back out to the chat room where I found him. Messages scroll like syrup at this hour. Thick and slow. A couple of the handles are obvious newbs with how much personal shit they're laying out in the open forum. DeathByRequest is not online, but he hasn't left the server completely. There's still hope.

Hope for what, I'm not quite sure. The events at his apartment are still fuzzy in my mind, but I do remember he demanded I leave. That isn't exactly a new thing—hookups don't always turn into an all-night cuddle fest. But what's new is that after such a rebuke, I still want to see him.

It's like being on new meds. That first couple of weeks when things shift. Your vision clears. Life seems bearable. Maybe even worth living.

I stare at the text box, swallow that tart morning-after taste I can't seem to shake, and compose a thousand different messages in my mind. The cursor blinks, waiting for instructions.

Finally, I type.

I want to see you again.

Shit. I don't even know his name.

But I hit send, anyway.

CHAPTER FIVE

I stay in possession of my faculties throughout the night and into the next day, and every moment is a fresh hell. At first the torture is only mental. Images flash in my imagination, and I slowly piece together the atrocities the zhelani has forced my hands to commit. The murders of the past year come to me in fragments. A scream echoes in my memory, and perhaps I can piece it together with a grunt or the sensation of the knife sliding into a woman's gut. The images do not tell a clear story, and if the zhelani enters me again soon, I won't have to remember at all.

But the creature sits at the bottom of its tank. More still than I've ever seen it. Even the bell-like chime it emits has grown faint.

Along with the images, there is the inevitable headache that splits from brain to spine whenever the creature is not in me. The vomiting is a mere inconvenience.

I sleep and wake with the grit of stale cotton in my throat and an absolute craving for that horrendous creature. I stumble to the living room and curl up on the couch. It's not just images anymore. My shaking hands remember the resistance of flesh and give of organs. I don't want to know how lungs feel when they are pierced or what happens when a heart stops before the knife is withdrawn.

My teeth clench, and I stare at the tank, wondering why the zhelani has left me this time. It has left me before. Usually just after a kill when it becomes too massive for me to hold. Occasionally, it has left me to punish me. I may not be able to communicate with it, but I know when it wants me to hurt.

True, I didn't kill this woman. But usually ... usually ... I can't follow the thought. Something feels different, as if the creature is not only punishing me but rejecting me. There is something final in the way it settles in its tank, keeping its hum low and distant. Even when it leaves me, I can usually hear its distant chime that vibrates me to the core. Now my body is silent. There is no echo of vibration. Everything hurts, and my body craves the bliss that comes when the zhelani takes over my body and pushes my thoughts to the edge of my mind.

I want it, in all its oblivion.

As if it can sense my desire, the zhelani curls in on itself. It churns in the tank, thick black turning purple where it swallows itself.

I beg myself not to go to it. For once, be strong. Don't even look at it. But my knees shift forward, my spread palms clutch the floor, and I drag myself towards the zhelani.

"You want another." I tap the glass. The sludge presses against the spot where my greasy finger hits. "I can get you another. A junky. They always want a way out. We can get one right now, down by the pier."

The sound of carnival rides comes to me, but it isn't the new mechanical music of the boardwalk. It's something older. Winding and cranking with the sound of barkers blending together. Five cents a ride. Five cents a show. Peek inside.

I don't want to see inside.

The zhelani sloshes. The stiff liquid throws itself at the glass, and an image of the woman flashes in my mind. She's spread-eagled on the couch and I'm ramming my fingers into her, curling and pulling out so viciously that it should hurt, but she's undulating to meet each stroke. "The woman? You want ..." I rack my brain and a name comes forth like all the other vomit these past two days. "Emma."

Saying her name loosens the zhelani's grip on me. A sharp pain shoots through my head. That pain should sound soft like a chime. It once had the roundness of a bell. Now it's all point and jab. And memory.

I remember her in the tunnels. The zhelani likes the dampness of the tunnels. It's at home in the wet darkness. So many of its victims have ended there. But she was pressed against the wrong wall, trembling in her defiance. In that moment, the zhelani had whipped in me, cutting my insides with a thousand hairline blades. Yes. It wanted her. But not in a way I could recognize. It was frenzied, enlivening me in an altogether new way. Even now, it transmits that straining need to me.

"Please don't make me," I say. "She doesn't want to die."

The splitting pain softens. It turns to a buzzing. A vibration. The smallest hint of pleasure. I inhale and give a sigh of relief. It expands further, the vibrations popping like soda bubbles. The zhelani calls to me like a mother reaching her arms open to accept an injured child.

I stand up. My body feels light. A roll of pleasure trickles down my spine, spreading out, past my skin, pulling me into the cool of the apartment.

"Yes," I sigh. "Thank you."

In the back of my mind, a chime drowns out the chorus of carnival barkers. I lean over the tank and open my mouth.

As the zhelani fills me, I sense the slightest hint of what it wants. Over the years it has asked for blood and bruises, humiliation and power. But now, the way it fills my crevices, I know, and I can finally say ... it wants another body.

CHAPTER SIX

The rest of the day is filled with a sort of peace. I've shot my shot and things are out of my hands. The satisfaction that comes when I've done everything in my power is its own intoxication. I return to my work and, though it's no more fulfilling than it was a few hours ago, I concentrate enough to finish three tasks and make headway on a fourth.

I force myself to wait until I'm home to check for a reply, but when I eventually open the program, there's nothing from him. Sitting on my couch with my laptop open and a glass of tonic next to me, I feel utterly alone. It's not a new sensation, but it's deeper and more intense than it's been in years. For one night, I was seen. I was touched. I felt *real*. And now, it's been taken from me. Again. A single hot tear rolls down my cheek. I rub the saltiness along my chin, sniff, and take two long gulps of the tonic, my blood racing from the bitter quinine of the imagined cocktail.

It's fine. Expected. I'm too old to blubber like a teenager.

Another gulp. I wish the cocktail was real and could deliver the oblivion I used to chase. But it's not worth it. He's not worth it.

My phone pings, yanking me out of my spiral with a violent tug of hope.

My public profile has a message request. I check his picture six times. Same slender nose and forest green eyes. My stomach flutters just looking at his sharp features. Remembering his hand in my pants, my own fingers creep down my stomach to the edge of my waistband as I hit accept.

I wait, but no message comes. No dots. Nothing.

My hand stops its downward migration. I finish off the rest of my tonic before I settle enough to compose a message, secretly hoping that in the time it takes me to swallow, he'll make the first move. But he doesn't.

I left my panties at your place. Can I get them back?

I stare at the question, delete it, then type it again and hit send before I can chicken out. We both know a pair of panties isn't worth my dignity.

CHAPTER SEVEN

We've reached an understanding, and the zhelani doles out a measure of ecstasy. Tension eases from me as it slithers in my chest and stomach.

A body.

The thrill of the boardwalk seeps through my shut window, but it no longer carries that bitter sorrow I've grown accustomed to swallowing. The screams and laughter swirl in towards something bigger. Hopeful. I stumble to open the window and squint in the bright sunlight reflecting off the glittering ocean. I inhale the salty air.

Not another death.

Seagulls caw and waves crash and I tilt like I'm walking on a ship as I make my way to the softness of my bed. I hum with satisfaction, echoing the sound that's finally returning to my companion, and fall into the blankets. Within me, the zhelani expands. It fills my body and stretches me. I become cavernous.

Not a knife rending guts from flesh.

I lie in bed and touch my thumbs to each fingertip. Waves of pleasure cascade down my digits, through my palms, numbing my arms. The creature vibrates through me, taking my awareness with it to realms unknown to other humans. In the moments when my wits return, I wonder where it is that this creature takes me. We travel far in an instant—I get a sense of space—but there is no destination. All around me is nothing but an inky expanse. Cool and damp, and terrifying in its strangeness. The ether of the universe or perhaps beyond? My companion moves through me, and it feels impossible, as if it should not even exist. In a way, it's a miracle. In a way, I'm grateful.

Another host.

I try to picture Emma. My companion. It has been so many years since I've had ... but the zhelani pushes that thought from me, gently, gently, just as it has pushed Emma's face from my mind. It has pushed everything from me. I am empty and echoing with the zhelani's pulsing desire. More, more, more. Its usual drumbeat. But beneath and between a more desperate hunger.

My eyes open to a dark room. Not the complete darkness that I've been swimming in, but the dull, flickering dark of night. I've lost track of time again.

I sigh, my body coming back to me. It doesn't hurt anymore. The zhelani has taken away my pain. My mind touches the edges of past and future, but it won't give me those. Not until I've followed through on my part of the dark deal we have somehow negotiated.

I laugh, my stomach ballooning out with the motion. Bargained? With the zhelani? Impossible. I belch, swallowing a sudden twist of impatience in my throat.

My phone rests on my nightstand. I pull it to me and squint as the screen unlocks, too bright and sudden. I can't log into the chat room through my phone, but finding Emma's social media is impossibly easy. The zhelani guides my hands, calling information to my eyes and fingertips as if by magic. Within moments—or hours, it's all the same—I find Emma, send her a friend request, and let the phone drop to my belly.

I want to reach down for the upright cock just beyond my bare stomach, but the zhelani stays my hand.

Wait.

The command echoes like thunder, clenching my jaw and curling my toes. Still, I try to reach for myself. I want pleasure. I deserve pleasure. I've been nothing but a loyal servant. My nerve endings scream, my cock leaps and strains to meet my hand, but it's useless.

The phone on my nightstand pings and I open one eye to look at it. I want to ignore the message, but my hand moves anyway, jerky and clumsy as it reaches for the phone. I exhale and surrender.

Saturday morning. Crispin Cafe.

I've got another day of just me and the zhelani. Another day before it will force my hand to do unspeakable things.

Memories surface, floating near my consciousness. The knife in my hand; hot blood pouring over my skin, warming my numb fingers.

I give a whimper as the zhelani twists inside me, releasing the memories and taking me back to oblivion.

CHAPTER EIGHT

The ecstasy of the weekend has left my body. My cells have stopped vibrating. I know this sensation too well. It's two weeks into a new SSRI, when things balance out and the sunshine becomes dim again. It's the day after taking MDMA. Apparently it's half a week after fucking a serial killer.

He suggests meeting at a coffee shop downtown, a train ride away for both of us and not directly between our neighborhoods. He's still being cautious, which is fair. He had planned to kill me just a few days ago, and for all I know he already has someone else lined up. This man, if he is who he says he is, has killed nearly a dozen people, and the well-lit public meeting spot is safest for me. But there's a tinge of disappointment, because the things my body craves cannot be done in public.

I've got that sort of hangover, sloshy feeling in my head as I walk through the door and scan the faces for his. I wish he'd asked me back to his place. I want to cocoon in his room and let my skin go numb. I want to lose track of time and days fucking him. I don't want to chat over coffee or ask how his day has been. But there he is, sitting at a small, round table near the back. In public.

I pause, savoring the sensation of desire—the way it puckers my skin and tingles in my brain. This is what I've been chasing with all the pills and therapy. It's what I couldn't find in nightclubs or sex parties—the ability to want.

His gaze stays planted firmly on me as I make my way to him. I feel him taking in each of my steps and the sway of my hips. Under his scrutiny, my motion becomes awkward to my own body. He makes me too self-aware, and in that awareness I'm wet again, nipples hard, throat aching. The vitality aches, like the exposed quick of a nail, something that should be hidden. Protected. And yet I can't help offering it to him.

"Hello." I sink into the chair across from him. Only once I'm safely supported do I allow myself to take him in. His broad shoulders are covered in a cream, cable-knit sweater that almost blends into his skin, making his dark stubble and forest-green eyes stand out stark on his face. "Thanks for meeting up with me."

He smirks. "You look well."

I flush. At home I had drawn out almost my entire closet, trying on every piece of clothing before settling on a slightly-too-tight skirt, tank top, and my trusty cardigan. Nothing seemed to fit right or look good enough, and it made me realize that for months I haven't cared how I look. I showered in extra-hot water, soaping twice and letting myself enjoy the feel of lather sliding over my skin. Anticipation of him woke me in a way I could barely remember. Maybe I have never felt this alive.

"It's polite to say thank you when someone compliments you," he says, chiding me like a child.

I give a low chuckle and decide to play whatever bullshit game he's playing. "Thank you."

He doesn't seem amused, but he doesn't demand more sincere gratitude. He takes a small package out of a satchel by his feet. It's brown paper, tied with string, and I instantly love his attention to detail.

I pick up the package. The light paper crinkles beneath my touch. "My panties? Thanks for the discretion."

"You don't sound thankful." His tone remains completely flat, difficult to read.

"Should I be?" I'm tired of his game and feel like a sullen teenager, wanting to provoke him into an emotional reaction. "It's common decency."

A flicker of amusement crosses his eyes, and for a moment I think I've won. "I don't want you to be thankful."

I furrow my brow, then feel a light trace of his fingertips at the hem of my skirt. His fingers are delicate, and the touch is slow and sure as it creeps beneath the fabric. I swallow down any retort I might have been thinking of.

"If you're grateful, you should pick up that package and leave." His fingers tippy-tap my inner thigh, spreading my legs. He leans in, as if we're having a serious conversation, reaching further up my leg until he finds the edge of my panties. "But I think you want something more than what I tied up for you."

As if to prove his point, he hooks the tip of one finger into the edge of my underwear and gives a gentle tug, barely enough to pull the fabric away from my wetness. Instead of squirming away from his touch, my body moves towards it, willing him to dip his fingers in further, to split my lips and feel my slickness.

"Yes. You definitely want something more." He removes his hand, trailing his fingers over the top of my thigh and squeezing my knee. "Let me tell you honestly. You should take the package and go."

Without his touch, I feel naked. A blush creeps into my cheeks, and I look around the coffee shop for signs that someone noticed our indiscretion. A single man near the front of the shop looks away quickly, but beyond him, we don't seem to have caught anyone's attention.

"If I don't?" I murmur. The words stick in my too-wet throat.

His thin lips twitch into the slightest frown and, for a moment, he's just a pathetic man hunched over a cafe table, thin to the point of gauntness, leaning in desperately towards a woman he barely knows.

I blink and the image is gone. Once again he's powerful and magnetic and his lips morph into a smile. "Open the package."

My heart beats faster. "Here? Now?"

"Here and now."

He waits. His eyes don't move from my face, as if he has all the time in the world for me. All the patience. What's the harm in flashing a pair of panties to a bunch of strangers? I realize this was planned—that's why he chose a coffee shop that neither of us frequent. A grin splits my lips. What else does he have planned?

I pull the package back, sliding it off the table.

He clicks his tongue on the roof of his mouth and gives a sharp shake of his head. His hand darts to my wrist, quick as a snake, and pinching as bad as fangs. The scab from my last night with him opens beneath the pressure, and a thin strip of bright red contrasts with the brown. "On the table."

I fight the urge to yank my wrist away and instead let him guide my hand back into the center of the table. Is this what desire feels like? The willingness to take risks? To suffer shame? The ability to feel shame at all? I set my jaw and keep my eyes locked on his as I find the edge of the string and pull. The twine falls away and I slide my forefinger beneath the flap of the wrapping, loosening the tape and opening the package.

Inside are my panties from the other night. At first glance, neatly folded into quarters, they are inconspicuous—just dark turquoise cotton overlaid with lace flowers. When I'm wearing them, they sit snug around my hips, and follow the curve of my butt. But when they're not on me, they're just dark fabric lying on a coffee shop table. I look into his eyes again, half-defiant and half-waiting for more instructions.

"Good." His voice is so low I have to bend towards him to catch his words. "Now, Emma, tell me what you want."

My eyebrows furrow and I trace the edge of the lace. "What I want?"

"Yes. You messaged me because you want something, right? Something more than the panties. What do you want?"

A dry bark of a laugh escapes my throat. "You know ..."

"I do." He licks his lips and draws his lower lip into his mouth, biting down on it. I squirm in my seat, my eyes locked to the soft nibble of his teeth. "I want to hear you say it, though."

The large coffee shop seems to shrink, and it feels like everyone is pressing in against me, waiting to hear me speak. I've never been one for dirty talk. I lean further over, and my thigh brushes his. I fill my lungs and exhale loudly. I can do this. "I want you to fuck me."

"Is that it?" He shakes his head, slow to the left, then the right. "I don't think so. It isn't me that you want. I'm just a man. A person who happens to have a cock that can slit into you. But you've done that. Plenty. You want something more."

I haven't thought beyond my desire for him. I just know our last time together left me unfinished. I want his cock in me, and I want to feel his body tighten with orgasm. My mind scrambles for more details. "I want to be naked on your bed, my legs spread wide. I want you to thrust slowly into me, inch by inch. I want ... I want you to drive me to ecstasy, until I shudder and clench around you. Then I want you to come inside me."

Inside me? My face turns bright red. It's a lie. I don't let men finish inside me. Except, waiting for his answer, it's the truth. My hands shake, hoping for a yes.

"Your body speaks even as your mind doesn't know what you're asking. Let me rephrase the question. Why do you want these things?"

My breath is coming short. I stare at him. He's not exactly attractive. His skin is smooth—unmarred, as if he skipped the acne of puberty. His shoulders are wide, pressing against his sweater. His eyes are the best part of him. That dark green almost swirls as I stare at them. I swallow. Locking gazes with him is like falling into a deep forest pool, cool and refreshing and without end. I drink of him. An image of him holding my still-beating heart flashes in my mind, and I realize there is more than one way a heart can be held. "I want to feel alive."

Shame immediately washes over me. The other side of wanting to feel alive is an admission that I don't. It's letting him know that I'm filled with decay that needs to be swept away, either by death or passion.

He doesn't nod. He barely even moves his lips when he says, "Pick up your panties. Put the crotch between your teeth. I will stand up to leave. You will follow five steps behind me."

Before I can protest, he pushes his chair back and strolls towards the door. He doesn't look back to see what I do. One step. I fondle the edge of the panties. Two steps. This is absurd. I'm not going to walk through a coffee shop with dirty underwear in my mouth. Three steps. He's a serial killer. Best to get out while I still can. Four steps. But the way he made me feel last time. Five steps. The way I still feel, watching the breadth of his shoulders and that minuscule movement beneath the fibers.

I grasp the crotch of my panties and stuff them between my teeth. Last week's desire comes through stale and sour, nearly making me gag. My eyes water, and I'm not sure whether it's with disgust or shame. I stand up and follow him, careful to keep five steps between us, hating him for his languid stride, but wanting him more with every step I take. I pick up my head. Throw my shoulders back. The man in the window is looking again. Two women in a corner whisper to each other. The barista stares, mouth agape. I look each of them in the eyes and follow him out of the shop.

Once I pass through the door, he grabs me by the waist, taking me away from the entrance a step, and rips the panties from my mouth. My teeth clink hard together, sending a shiver of pain down my spine. But the sensation fades in the heat of his kiss—hard enough to draw blood from my lips— and I surrender to his advance, half hoping he will fuck me there, on the sidewalk, as people pass by.

"My place. Tonight. Nine o'clock," he whispers in my ear.

Then he's gone, and I'm sinking down to scoop up the panties he left on the sidewalk.

CHAPTER NINE

Disgust pulses through me even as the zhelani swells with satisfaction. I put my hands in my jean pockets and furrow my brow like the old man I should be. My shuffling steps lead me the long way home, down by the boardwalk. It's gotten cold enough that most of the rides are shut down during the week, but even the gentle hum of the machines at the few open food stalls calms my anger.

As close as I live to the boardwalk, I've never been to it while it was open. In the long hours before morning, when I could pick up a mark, sure. But never in broad daylight. The scents and sounds have been a distant hum that floats through my window, as dark and pulling as the zhelani's music.

I realize that every city we've gone to—always a city, never a town, never the rural spaces in-between—has had a functioning boardwalk or fairground. These sounds that make me pick up my feet and cock my head have been my backdrop for the past century. A few lazy shucks of skee-balls and the false cheer of a carousel, somewhere between a music box and a march. I catch the scent of roasting hot dogs and my eyes close.

Memories rise in me as slick as vomit. It wasn't a boardwalk. It was a carnival. The people were crushing in and the sun blistered down. And my hand ... the softness it held.

My breath catches and I cry out with a soft moan.

Something's off. I can feel the zhelani consolidating its mass and itching at my throat. I'll barely make it home before it demands I expel it. I'm so used to the murders, when it clings to my innards. Right now it should be rising in me—filling me. I should be vibrating with anticipation. Hell, I shouldn't be able to think.

But this is altogether new. My consciousness breaks through the mists of a hundred-year fog, and I question the creature that usually puppets me so easily.

I grasp a brass railing and lean into the lull of the nearly empty carousel. One child playing hooky. A couple touching noses.

A couple ...

My knuckles go white. The sound lifts me, as if it's trying to draw me from my body. It's the complete opposite of the existence I've grown accustomed to—the hours and days and years when the zhelani sinks me deep into myself, opening expanses in my cells, introducing me to universes within. This is without, and it tugs at my mind and heart.

My stomach heaves and I bite my lip, stumbling away from the noise and memories.

When we get home I lock the door and draw the curtains. The zhelani pulls me to its tank as if a cord is attached between my belly button and the glass, and my body follows behind like a rag doll. The creature expels itself from my mouth in a soft, bulky string. I don't even retch, just let it slip out. What was once a contest of wills has become routine.

Only when I'm empty and weak do I pick up the knife.

The bone handle barely sings against my palm. The chimes are distant. I furrow my brow and lean close to the tank. The creature is small. Weak? It shrinks away from me and my breath fogs the glass.

I consider giving it a taste of my blood. A peace offering of sorts. But no. The zhelani can't feed off of its host. I've learned that much.

There's nothing to do but wait in silence and see what exactly it has planned for this woman.

CHAPTER TEN

Time drags. If I was at work, I could at least distract myself with data tables and code. Something to solve. This anticipation can't be calculated away.

When I return home, my apartment feels dingier than when I left. Over the past year I've let dust collect in corners and on shelves. Clothes are everywhere, in various states of washing. There always seem to be dishes in the sink even though I can't remember the last time I ate. I pinch the roll of fat at my belly. I eat. I must. But without pleasure, there's no memory.

The urge to clean strikes me. I open the curtains and let sunshine sterilize my home.

He asked what I wanted. I can't remember the last time someone asked that. It feels so good to be pressed for more—like a grape. He squeezed out my answers and tonight we'll turn them into wine.

I begin the drudging process of tidying. The apartment could use a deep scrub, but before I can get to carpets and tiles, I have to put away the belongings that have escaped their homes over the past ... year? Two? How long has it been since I've been able to face my mess? I end up sorting the junk drawer on the kitchen floor. Like an archaeologist, I find hints of the past five years in layers. Except instead of clay pots and bones, my life is measured in half-finished packets of pills. Here are the antipsychotics my psychiatrist insisted would get my anxiety under control. And here are the four different kinds of antidepressants, each showing a varying degree of effort based on the popped out pills and scratchy foil on the backs. No matter how bad things were—or maybe because things were so bad—I never found one I could commit to.

I consider calling my psychiatrist. Adjusting my meds again. I even make an event in my calendar. I'll call on Monday. Things will be better this time, because something has shifted in me.

I want.

I spend the afternoon and early evening hours moving items from one box to another. Then another. No wonder I felt suffocated beneath all this stuff. And dust. My eyes water and I give in to multiple fits of sneezing before the orange tint in the window fades to gray and it's time to leave.

When I exit the subway, I'm afraid I'll get the wrong street or mix up the low, fat buildings. But my feet carry me as if I've been going to this apartment my whole life. Exactly at nine, I knock on his door.

"Emma." The serial killer swings open the door and steps to the side. "Come in."

I step over the threshold into his domain. He wears the same sweater, but seems thinner. His cheeks almost sink in, and his body swims in the thick wool. He steps forward, arms spread, and almost shyly covers my mouth with his. It is nothing like the possessive kiss at the coffee shop. His lips are soft and tender, and though there's nothing wrong with the kiss except a little too much spit, I'm hungry for the man he was this morning.

When he pulls away, he stares down at me. His eyebrows pinch together and he gestures to the couch. "Shall we?"

"I ... don't even know your real name," I say. His profile had called him DeathByRequest. When I was looking for death, that had been enough, but now I want something more. I try to laugh, but the rush of air sounds more like a bark than the playful giggle I intend.

Countering my boisterousness, he releases a sigh. "D is fine."

I cross my arms. "You're really sticking with the whole death thing?"

He lowers his eyes, his shoulders slumping. "My name is Daniel. People used to call me D. I don't spend much time with people who need to know my name these days, but I suppose D will still suffice."

He gestures to the couch again, no more insistent than the first time, but pity moves my feet. His loneliness echoes my own. I cross in front of him. My knees, which were jelly before he opened the door, now seem locked into place. Everything feels stiff. I try not to wobble as I cross the small living room and he closes the door behind me. I don't sit, though.

"Do you want to go to your bedroom?"

He gives that exhausted sigh again, and I'm almost offended. I know I've been chasing him shamelessly, but he could at least make some effort.

"Maybe I had the wrong idea. I can go."

"No. Stay. Please." He looks at me with those green eyes, this time clouded by a deep, longstanding pain. My mouth forms a small oh of recognition and I sink to the couch.

"I wasn't prepared." He waves a hand down his body. "I guess I thought you wouldn't come."

"Did you not want me to?" I ask. I'm not prepared for vulnerability. It's easy enough to complain that there isn't enough connection in a digital-first world, but it's something altogether different to experience intimacy. My stomach goes queasy and I realize that somewhere between my final semesters of university and the soulless years of data entry, I've forgotten how to talk to people.

"It's not about what I want. It hasn't been about that for years."

"Years? You can't be much older than me." Have we reached the age when we start judging our lives in years instead of semesters or seasons?

"I'm older than I look." As he speaks, he peels his sweater off. "Just give me a minute to get ready."

A line of hair extends from his belly button into the waistband of his pants, and I imagine where the hair goes. What it covers. Where it ends. My anticipation returns, until D turns and I see his back.

Angry white scars crisscross over his flesh, leaving no shades of pink. It's all gray and white, lacing over itself.

I inhale sharply.

"A lot to take in?" he asks as he approaches the aquarium. "Don't worry, it doesn't hurt."

Suddenly, I'm very worried. Days ago, I was willing to let this man murder me, but I never agreed to torture.

He leans over the aquarium, his sharp nose close to the black liquid, which is so dark it shimmers purple in some places. My head fills with images of the previous night. He vomited something into the tank. Other parts are still unclear, but I'm sure of that memory.

Now, the liquid draws itself up to D's lips with what looks like a tentacle that forms from the jellied liquid, then passes limb after limb into his waiting mouth. D shudders. His back swells. The scars crack, letting shimmery black ooze drip down his blemished skin. It flows and then hardens into a pulsing shell.

"What is that?" I ask.

But he can't answer with his jaw practically unhinged as he swallows more and more of the liquid.

"D?" I whimper and hate the weakness of my voice.

He turns. His face no longer has that gaunt appearance, and his biceps have filled out, although a bit unevenly and purple, like the beginning of a bruise. The color spreads down his chest, racing towards the line of hair I had been admiring a few short moments ago.

"Get undressed," D commands. His voice has the steady sureness it had this morning and the intensity of our first encounter, as if he's holding back unbridled power.

"That's some kind of foreplay." I mean for it to sound like a joke, but a squeak betrays my fear.

"You want this." It isn't a question but a reminder.

What's most fucked up is that even with everything I just saw and memories of our first night flooding back into me, he's right. I do want this. I want him, and I think I want whatever just crawled into his body. Something thuds in my chest, echoing my heart, trying to get at this man.

I obey his command. First, I shrug my sweater over my head, then wiggle the skirt off my legs. My thighs and belly relax, freed of the tight fabric. Next I lift my shirt, revealing a lace bra which snaps off easily enough. My breasts give a small bounce as they fall into place, then swing low as I bend to peel off my tights and underwear.

The room is cool, and prickles run up my forearms. I stand naked before D, and he lets his eyes graze my body from toes to ankles, knees, thick thighs, cunt covered in a patch of fur, rolling belly, plump tits, and a long neck. He settles on my face. "You're beautiful."

My head shakes by reflex.

"Don't do that. I get to say what I find beautiful." He approaches me and lifts my hand in his, pulling my arm out to better survey me. "You're strong. Your body is awake and vibrant. You are beautiful. And the zhelani likes you."

I resist the urge to shake my head again. "The zhelani?"

He moves in close and traces kisses down my neck, pushing that strange word from my mind. My nipples pucker in response, and he guides me onto the couch until I'm lying flat, my legs dangling off the edge, and the weight of him pressing on top of me. His lips move down my collar bone, circling one breast, then the other. His tongue darts out to flick a nipple, and I moan, but he doesn't stop to pursue my pleasure. Instead he continues his investigation of my body. He suckles on the spaces between my ribcage, nibbles around my belly button, and licks the crevices between my thighs. My hands reach to his hair, gripping its thickness, but he guides them back to the cushions as he continues down my thighs to my knees. He swirls his tongue around my ankle bones, then kisses my feet and leaves dry pecks on my toes.

"Close your eyes."

I close my eyes, and the heat of his body leaves me. I hear the rustle of his pants as he removes them, and I want to lift my head and see him in his full nakedness—to assess him as he assessed me. But I keep my eyes closed. If that's what it takes to get him inside me, I'll obey.

He nudges my thighs apart, and I pull my heels on to the couch. As the hot tip of his penis strokes my lips apart, my eyes flutter open.

I make out a dark shape before he claps his hand over my eyes and I'm back in darkness.

D enters me, and it's a practice in patience to not buck up to meet him. The warmth of his skin is exquisite, and the pumping of his blood hardens his cock against the soft folds of my flesh. I clench my buttocks to keep my body still on the couch, letting him enter me as slowly as he wants.

It feels like he could continue separating me forever, and I only know he's reached the entirety of his depth from the warmth of his pelvis against mine. I release a moan that vibrates in the sweet spot between pleasure and pain, and rotate my hips to give full harbor to him.

"Emma," he echoes back to me. His voice sounds deeper with my eyes closed—a bass that fills the vaulted ceilings of the drafty room.

"D," I answer. He moves in me, not quite rhythmically, but with enough regularity for me to anticipate each stroke and rise to meet him.

"You want this," he repeats.

"Yes," I agree, moaning into his tangle of hair that falls on my face. He's still covering my eyes, and I'm starting to see bright patches of light from the pressure. Stars glow green, then pink, then yellow. Finally, they burst. The colors fall over me like molten liquid, and my pussy pulsates around D's cock.

"Yes," he whispers, slowing long enough for the grip of my shivering pussy to subside, then ramping back up, preparing me for another wave of pleasure.

He's not only above me, but all around me. I'm smothered by him, and it's a delicious sensation, like I'm floating along a lazy river, hot in the summer sunshine. The vision in the back of my eyelids grows again, expanding until it explodes as if he's creating tiny universes inside me.

Yes. This is what I wanted. This is what I dreamed possible.

I no longer have to speak. He seems to know every time my soul screams yes.

He removes his hand, but I keep my eyes closed, seeking the bright spots amidst the black backdrop—each one expanding like its own galaxy. Spinning faster and faster. It's unimaginable and yet it's happening within me. I cry out, but his mouth covers mine. Instead of kissing me, he exhales into me, expanding my ribcage so that my hard nipples rub against the light dusting of fur on his chest.

I moan on the exhale, and then he breathes into me again, his hips pressing against me as his air fills my lungs.

I'm light in the ecstasy of the moment, as if I'm standing atop a mountain, looking down on the entire world, and it's all within my reach.

On the third breath, he doesn't remove his mouth. We rebreathe the same air until there's no oxygen left to share and I grow dizzy.

I'm about to open my eyes and beg for a break when a stilted cry escapes his lips and he slams his pelvis against mine, his cock hitting the most sensitive areas inside me and making me yelp in surprise.

The liquid that fills me is hot and unending. I squirm away from the scalding heat, but his weight has me pinned. It's so hot. I'm burning inside like the wet heat of a forest fire, and it smolders and smokes but doesn't stop.

The pulsing is as rhythmic as D's movements were, and it continues, coaxing another orgasm from me, until I turn the couch beneath us wet, trying to extinguish his fire.

D collapses on top of me, then rolls to the side, wedged between the back of the couch and my vibrating body.

"You okay?" he breathes. His voice is high and tinny. The deep bass that had so attracted me to him is gone, as is the buzzing of the moment between us.

I nod but don't open my eyes. "That was amazing."

He kisses my cheeks and whispers so quietly that I must misunderstand, but I think he says, "I'm sorry."

When I finally open my eyes, there's no denying the change in D. It's not only that he feels feather-light against me, but he looks emaciated, as if he hasn't eaten in months. His skin has turned pasty white again, no sign of the purpling. My hand brushes the scars on his back, and they are dry, no longer weeping.

I wiggle out from beneath him and sit up, searching for my clothes. This time, I'm determined not to leave my panties behind.

As I'm shimmying my skirt over my thighs I look to him, then to the empty aquarium. Then back to him. Understanding slowly dawns on me.

"No." Even as I protest, a sick satisfaction churns inside of me. I had begged for it, but my desire is replaced by horror at the slick movement in my belly.

He sits up on the other end of the couch and hangs his head in his hands, his fingers tangling in his mess of hair. His silence is as thick as the liquid had been.

I reach out and touch his shoulder, which moves like paper over his bones. "D? What's wrong?"

"It's gone." He finally lifts his head and his eyes brim with tears.

"What's gone?"

His wide eyes settle on me. "The zhelani." His voice breaks. "You ... you took it all."

I back away and give an awkward smile. "I didn't take anything."

My gaze flits to the aquarium again.

"I need it." He launches off the couch, but I sidestep and he falls to the floor with a sickening thud. He lifts himself on his arms, and gazes up at me. "Please."

I pull my shirt angrily over my head and take another step away from him. "Look, I don't know what you're playing at ..."

Except I do. My body is beginning to buzz. My mind is practically bursting. It's this weekend. It's this week. But it's a hundred times stronger.

"It wasn't supposed to be this way," he says.

"What way?" I ask through a clenched jaw.

He looks at me with sunken eyes, black shadows dancing beneath them. They barely look green anymore, more of a muddy brown, turning black. His vitality is fading.

"You were supposed to be ..." He breaks off in a whimper. "We were ... supposed to be partners."

I try to summon sympathy for the creature kneeling in front of me, but pleasure pulses inside me, dancing me towards euphoria. I feel full, nearly bursting, and my fingertips tingle until I run them lightly over the fabric of my skirt, then they sing.

"You're feeling it, aren't you?" He asks sullenly, dropping his gaze. His open mouth is a gaping hole, and I can't look at him.

"Shh." I hold my hand up, no longer shy or submissive. He's no more than a wrong choice at a club. It just happens that the club was the dark web and he was a choice of serial killer rather than fuck boy. Or maybe a bit of both. I stand up, take one look at the leather of his skin holding his bones together, then leave.

CHAPTER ELEVEN

The way that woman looked at me. Not even pity. Disgust. Her eyes, which had stared at me with such fierce hunger, went flat, and she turned away. Practically fled the apartment. And I can't blame her.

I can feel the way my skin hangs from my bones, as if I'm a deflated balloon. Nothing is left in me. Not a drop of the creature that has sustained me all these years.

She carries the zhelani from my apartment, and every inch of movement tears at my guts. I try to stand, to follow, but collapse to the floor, bumping against the coffee table and bruising my now delicate, paper-thin skin.

I turn to my side and slowly push myself to sitting. The apartment looks different. Empty. I swear if I spoke, my voice would echo. But I don't speak. I pour a glass of whiskey and raise the amber liquid to my lips with a shaking hand.

I swallow the familiar warmth, letting it cauterize the wounds of the evening. It isn't how I planned. But the zhelani does what it wants. I've always known that.

There should be some sense of freedom or relief. The creature controlled me for so long, forcing my body to commit terrible crimes, then feeding me pleasure. Training me on pleasure and pain until I couldn't understand the difference. Blood was delicious. Death was better than sex.

I swirl the whiskey in my glass, watching it ripple, and remember the zhelani in its tank. I never understood why it would leave me. There was no pattern. Sometimes, it would surrender my body directly after a kill, basking in its own slush while I trembled at the fog of memories it left behind. Other times it would stay, and I would feel its digestion in my chest as it moved on itself in that semi-regular pattern of autophagia, always churning, never talking to me, unless you consider the silent suggestions of who and how to kill communication.

Another sip of whiskey and my nerves begin to settle. There's pain without the zhelani. Not just the loneliness in my mind, but a slow burning in my nerve-endings, as if I've come in from a cold day and my skin is cold to the touch but feels like its on fire.

I convinced myself the zhelani was shedding. Some sort of propagation. If I trusted the process, there would be two of us. Two hosts, two zhelani. The woman was attractive enough. I could live a life with her, and there'd be someone who understood what I'm going through.

But, no.

It left with her. Now only the smallest fragment remains in me. I can't feel its vibrations or hear the distant chiming that became my daily font. It wasn't procreating. It was moving on to a newer, younger body. One that doesn't ache like mine and feel so fucking hollowed out.

I sigh and pour another splash of whiskey. I'll have to go out and get food. When the zhelani is in me, there's no space for food. Now I'm going to have to relearn how to chew and swallow. How to cook.

How to live.

My head splits with a headache from hell and the room feels too bright. I stumble to my feet and turn off the lights, letting the moon illuminate the room. Still, it seems too bright. I close my eyes, but the pain isn't in my vision. It seeps down my entire body, crawling through me. A wave of ravenousness swells in me and, when it passes, I realize I'm biting my knuckles so hard I've drawn a few drops of blood.

I go for the towel in the kitchen. Remembering slicing Emma's wrist, I turn to the buffet.

The knife is still there.

I can get the zhelani back.

CHAPTER TWELVE

"You look different," are the first words out of Monica's mouth in the office on Monday. "New haircut? Makeup?"

My hair is the same shaggy bob I've always worn; the only time I put on makeup is when I'm going to a rave and won't care how smudged it gets. But I just shrug. "Nope. Nothing like that."

"The mystery man. You spent all weekend fucking, didn't you?"

It strikes me as funny that we're not friends and yet we can talk about fucking. I guess it's better than spreadsheets. I laugh. "Not quite."

It's the closest to truthful I've ever gotten with Monica, because honestly, I want to make sense of what happened.

Maybe what D and I did could be classified as fucking. We had sex, but whatever happened at the end, that was transcendence. He pulsed in me and the whole world pulsed around me, in and out of existence. It was exquisite.

While I didn't see him Sunday, I spent the day in bed, pulsating with whatever liquid he had pumped into me. I wanted to be disgusted by the undulations rippling below my skin, but the rolling pleasure was too intense, so I guess that day of lying in bed, not eating or drinking and only getting up to pee, could almost be considered sex as well. Not with D. Never again after seeing the shell of him when that black ooze left him. But it was like sex with whatever he left me. The way my lower belly clamped and the liquid that dripped from between my legs ... better than sex.

"Does he have a twin sister? If a weekend with him can do that ..." She waves a hand over her face, then gestures to mine.

"He didn't do anything," I say more sharply than I expect.

Monica's eyes go round and she pats the air as if to placate me. "Okay, no talking about the secret weekend lover. Got it. But seriously, you should consider getting bangs. You'd rock some fringe."

And just like that, we're back to socially safe topics.

Monica tries to engage me a few more times, but my one-word answers and grunts eventually turn her away. Even without Monica hanging around my desk, I can't concentrate though. It's different than last week when I was filled with anticipation, and it's definitely different than the past few months when I couldn't concentrate because I wanted nothing to do with the day to day life unfolding around me.

It took me most of Sunday to come to terms with what D left inside me. I didn't want to enjoy that foreign substance, but every time a wave of disgust washed over me it was followed by a ripple of ecstasy. Now the gurgling in my stomach is more manageable. When it slides down from my ribcage and rubs my clit from the inside, I cross my legs and rock back and forth, uncertain whether I'm urging it to stay put or move deeper in me.

A couple of times I excuse myself to the restroom and, locked in a stall, let it fill my skin. It pushes past my pussy, down my legs. My muscles shiver, then loosen, as if I've just run a race. My toes tingle, happily freezing in my socks. I might have to call out of work tomorrow.

Or the rest of my life. I have no idea what this thing is or how long it will take to get used to it wriggling through me. I can't imagine D had a job. Well, nothing beyond killing people and rustling through their bank accounts for loose change.

I flush even though I haven't urinated, then take my time washing my hands. I run my fingertips over my soapy skin. The water is cold, but heat emanates from within me. There's something more, too. A vibration, as if my cells have been charged with electricity.

I swallow and let out a long, low burp. I lean heavy on the sink, staring in the mirror, trying to find some trace of that oil slick in my eyes.

Today's going to be difficult.

———

Most of my day is spent in the restroom and, among other things, I conclude that the night cleaning crew isn't as thorough as necessary. The grout is dark with grime, and the tiles are slick with scum. I sit on the toilet, farting even though no shit comes out, and burping, the feeling of nausea making me draw the obviously underutilized bucket out from the cleaning closet and into the stall with me.

Three, maybe four times, I think about calling out sick—for the rest of the day or maybe the week. But if I'm not offing myself, I need the pay. There are car payments and rent due at the beginning of the month. Both reasons to stay at work, filling in data and checking it twice. A Santa Claus of spreadsheets.

It's towards the end of the day that I realize this sludge is changing me. And not just in the expanding and expelling sort of ways. My attention zeroes in on Craig, a slightly older colleague who sits two desks over. He's skinny, with a fashion sense somewhere between emo and hipster, and although I'm almost certain he wore braces when he was a kid, he could use another round. Most days I wouldn't notice him at all, but today I look at his dark freckles and tangle of red hair, and something flips in my chest. It isn't exactly attraction, at least not in a way I've felt before. If anything, the pimples along his cheeks and chin stand out more, the blood pressing puss against his skin and almost pulsating with his heartbeat. No. I definitely don't want to fuck him. But there's something about his proximity that heightens my senses. I want him. Not him in me. Not him doing things to me. Just, him.

The desire rising in me makes it almost impossible to sit still. I wiggle as if I have to pee, and wonder if I shouldn't run to the bathroom one more time just to be safe. But, no. It's Craig. I want to be skin-to-skin with him. I want to suck his soul from his body.

It's that last thought that terrifies me. It's the same thing D said to me that first night. Or something close to it. Something about extracting my soul from my cunt. In the moment, it was the kind of overdramatic metaphor that excited me. I had bucked closer to him, taunting him, begging him to make it happen. It didn't, of course. I'm still here, the same person I was. But there's no denying that there's something inside me, and it wants Craig of all people.

Slowly, almost painfully, I unseal my attention from Craig. But my office holds twenty-two people, and my newfound desire doesn't seen to discriminate based on age, skin color, or sex. Every time my eyes drift to the person sitting behind another desk, my chest jumps with longing, less like butterflies of lust and more like a fish flopping towards water. My eyesight narrows on the person. I sense their breathing. The pulse in their neck. The way they type and sigh or stretch their arms, revealing the tender skin at their wrists. It all feels too clear for me, and that's when I realize it must be the ooze D put in me. I don't want these people, it does, and if I'm to guess how it wants them, it prefers flayed.

I spend too much time in my internet browser instead of Excel. I look up the recent murders in the city.

There are more than I expect, but finding most of the ones from D is easy. He has a couple of tells. He took his victims to remote places. Five were found in the tunnels— enough that I'm surprised he wasn't nicknamed the Tunnel Terror. But the others are at the docks, on a quiet road north of town, and in abandoned buildings. Some are flayed. Some have crushed bones. Suffocated. The method is different, but the explicitness is similar. They were all slow, painful deaths. I suddenly know that they were all awake as he slowly drained their life from them. This creature doesn't live on blood or flesh. It craves pain.

My stomach twists so hard I almost vomit on my desk.

Yes, it tries to tell me.

It craves surrender.

CHAPTER THIRTEEN

Sometime in the past few days I made it from the living room to my bed, and now I can't find the energy to leave. I'm not eating, so I don't have to shit, but when I have to piss, I can barely crawl across the carpet, the fibers eating at my bare knees.

Pain racks my body. Calling it waves would be too generous. The ebbing is more than any human should be able to stand, and the flow. My God, the flow. My head spins and I try to vomit but nothing comes out. I will need to leave the apartment soon. Get some food in me. But right now that feels impossible—both the leaving and the eating.

This time I shove off the porcelain throne and come face-to-face with the mirror. I lean heavy on the counter, and my wrists send sharp needles up my arms from the weight of my upper body. I raise my eyes from the metal strip at the bottom of the mirror. My body takes blurry shape before me.

Skin hangs off my ribs. I shift my weight to one hand and pull at a fold with the other. The skin stretches two or three inches away from my body without resistance. Upon release, it sucks back with a wet slurping sound. I wince, more from the sound than the pain of it, but there is pain. All that exists is pain.

My collarbones protrude, threatening to break the skin that hangs from them like a wet sweater, reforming with every sway of my body. My cheeks are no better. The bags beneath my eyes are a purplish blue, heavy with blood.

"Fuck," I say and lean closer to inspect the spiderweb of red on my eyeballs. It looks like maybe a vein exploded, because a large dot takes up half of the white on my left eye. The right one is clearer, but its mapping of blood doesn't give me much hope.

I press my forehead against the cold mirror. A shiver traces through my spine and my teeth clench.

I close my eyes and try to remember the man I was before this creature found me. I was young. Twenty-something. I feel like I should remember that detail. I should remember every piece of my previous life but, like everything else, the creature has sucked my memory dry. Fine. Twenty-some-thing. Late twenties. Not yet thirty, though. Someone had been planning something for my birthday. A wife? Girl-friend? Hell, maybe my mother. A hundred years, and a man starts to forget, even without a parasite hellbent on sucking out his brain. Some woman. But I never made it to that birthday party. There were plenty of parties after that. I liked going into smokey nightclubs, high off a fresh kill. I liked the way the singer's voice vibrated to my core.

Now I sway to an imaginary tune. Yeah, I liked the blues, the beat always a stutter behind where it should be. The sway of it.

My hand slips and I stumble, but I catch myself before going down on the cold tile.

I look back in the mirror and try to find the man I was before the zhelani took me.

I raise an arm, the effort immense despite how stick-light

it is. I let my palm fall flat on the mirror and pain slushes down my limb. I like the way it feels. Real. It's been so long since I've felt anything beyond the alternating numb and bliss given to me by the zhelani.

I hit the mirror again.

And again. Harder.

Pain blossoms like fire in my palm.

Again.

Again.

The mirror cracks, a line running up the silver surface. I take a deep breath and look at my face cut in two, one half lower than the other.

I set my teeth. My tongue feels like a piece of dried jerky between them, and I suck on it, seeking flavor or texture—something outside of myself. But there's nothing. I'm alone.

The apartment is so quiet without the zhelani. The constant drone and occasional chiming of bells have become so ingrained in me that a world without its noise feels static, as if I'm moving through it but there's no time.

I'm back on my knees again, because looking at myself is impossible and walking is too difficult. I crawl to the living room. Further. Past the carpet line onto the hardwood floor. No sense in going to the kitchen; there's nothing to eat and I doubt the final beer will give me enough energy to do anything worthwhile.

"You absolute bastard," I grunt through clenched teeth.

I make it to the buffet. The tank's still there. Still empty. Next to it, the knife is still open.

I grab the bone handle, pull it open, and stare at the dark metal blade, etched with runes I've never understood. Not that I haven't tried to look them up. But the libraries and academics tossed my queries aside. Not serious. Nothing.

But they were something. That knife. Whether it or the

zhelani came first is muddled in my mind. But I know the two are tied.

My hand shakes as I line the blade up against a rib. All these years, and it never needed sharpening.

I let the inadequate weight of my arm pull the blade across my flesh.

My mind clears.

I was twenty-nine years old and Maddie was the one planning the party. But not just her. Mother and Auntie Gladys helped because ...

The memory fades, leaving only the pain of the open wound. I suck air between my teeth and force my body to calm itself. I will remember. I lift the knife again.

Maddie needed help because she was pregnant. We had been trying for years, and we were both thrilled even as she spent her first months vomiting morning and night. My birthday was in August; the baby was due in the fall. But none of that is important, because ... the important thing happened in late June when the weather was sweltering and all of us were going stir crazy with the lazy summer stillness.

Then ...

A carnival came. They set up their tents at the fairground just outside of town and Maddie begged me to take her. Mama said not to go—the excitement would be too much for her delicate condition. Auntie Gladys slipped me five dollars and told us to make a memory worth keeping. Maddie put her blonde hair in rollers and it fell soft and sweet around her shoulders and hell if she wasn't glowing, just like everybody said pregnant women did.

It was really happening. The family. The life we wanted.

I borrowed Father's car because I didn't want Maddie walking in the heat, and even then we didn't go until late afternoon when the sun was lower and the weather a little more forgiving. Mother warned Maddie to wear a shawl, to not breathe in too much of the fair-ground dust, and to come home early if she got tired, and of course Maddie promised. But as soon as we got in the car, things shifted. Maddie had always been that way—sugar in front of our parents and spice when she was alone with me.

"D, I'm having a baby, don't treat me like a child," she told me when we're bumping along in the car. I had slowed so much that we could have been walking faster. "Your mother babies me enough as it is. I don't need it from you, too."

I looked over at her all dolled up, at my knuckles white on the wide black steering wheel, then back at her. We shared a devilish grin, and I eased the gas pedal to the floor. I can feel the thought that went through my head that day: "that's my girl."

The parking lot was packed tight with cars when we arrived at the fairground, and we joked that we would have been just as well off parking at home. We had a certain holiday spirit about us, like we were back in elementary school and just released for summer break. Maddie got a thin film of sweat on her brow and her makeup smeared a bit, but she was all the more beautiful for it. That day—every day— she was perfect.

We walked pressed close together, my arm around her waist, pulling her here and there so we didn't get run over by an enthusiastic child or pushed by the parents chasing them. The late afternoon was comprised of laughter and amusement and the sun hung low and red for what felt like forever, as if the day refused to give way to the night. We split spun sugar, and I led her away from the rides, further down the midway, off to the side, where we could steal a moment of privacy.

In the shadow of a ramshackle tent, I moved close enough to feel her ragged breath on my cheek, and then I kissed her.

"No respect." A grating voice broke the tenderness rising

in the moment. "We're people, too. You know? We deserve some privacy."

An older woman waived her arm, sweeping across the tents, which were drab, olive green, not the colorful, striped tents we'd been passing all evening.

I broke apart from Maddie and stepped half in front of her, protecting her from this woman's anger. "Truly sorry, Ma'am. We didn't mean any harm."

"No harm, no harm, they never mean any harm." Her piercing green eyes clouded over, as if she was making some calculation. When they cleared, her entire demeanor shifted. She stood upright and pulled her white button-up shirt closed over her exposed cleavage. She threw down her lit cigarette butt and stomped it out, freeing her fingers to work the top button into place. "You're a good man. I can see. Got a good woman by your side."

I pushed Maddie further behind me, but she poked her head out from my shoulder and whispered, "D, I think she's a fortune teller," and I felt her excitement hot on my back and in her tightening grip on my bicep.

"Good eye, child," the old woman crooned. Her plain blue skirt and white blouse did not portray the colorful appearance of a fortune teller, but I gathered these were the carnie's private quarters, and off-the-clock she was an ordinary middle-aged woman. Or she tried to be.

"We don't need our fortune told," I said to Maddie. "Our future is flush."

The fortune teller stared at me, her eyes growing darker, like those of a forest. "You think so? You do. But that baby won't see the light. Heaven help his soul."

I took a step back and collided into the softness of Maddie's breasts and slightly swollen stomach. "Let's go Maddie."

Maddie gripped my bicep harder. "Let's listen to what she has to say. Maybe there's something she can do."

"She's just trying to scare you." I looked into Maddie's pleading eyes. I never could say no when she got like that. "Oh, fine. Maybe a reading wouldn't hurt."

The woman eyed us carefully, which probably would have been more foreboding if she was in her stage get up. But even with her in a skirt good enough for Sunday service, a chill wrapped round my neck. "Fifty cents. Each."

It was a rip off. Side-show attractions were supposed to be a dime each. But Maddie continued squeezing at me, urging me on. I pitied her. She couldn't even go on any rides. She deserved some fun, and if this is how she wanted to spend our money, I wasn't going to deny her. I dug in my pocket and handed over a dollar.

The woman contemplated the crumpled bill, then me. "I said each." She nodded at Maddie's stomach.

At this point, I was ready to cut my losses and get out of there, but Maddie clawed deeper into my forearm, leaving little half-moons in my tan skin, so I reached into my pocket and pulled out two quarters—the last of our money.

I hope this hack is worth it, I thought.

"I am," she answered.

I told myself she was bluffing. It's a thought any man would have had, and she's good at reading people. That's her job. I nearly had myself convinced she was nothing but a confidence artist but there was still a shiver of doubt as she turned and, instead of leading us to the fortune teller's tent on the midway, took us deeper into the personal tents. Around every corner, a hush fell on the half-dressed carnies. They slowed their actions and stared, and it felt like we were wading through molasses.

The fortune teller led us into a tent that looked the same as the ten we'd just passed. Inside was a cot, a trunk set up as a table with a deck of cards on the lid, and a single folding chair across from the cot. The woman settled on the cot and pointed to the chair, which Maddie collapsed into.

"I can't help your baby," the fortune teller said flatly. There was perhaps a flash of pity that smoothed the deep sun-wrinkles around her eyes. But before I could be sure, it was gone. She was staring at me with those forest-wise eyes, disregarding Maddie altogether.

"Then why—"

She held up a finger to cut me off. "Great tragedy will strike you. Soon. You'll lose everything. The pain will be immense. That, you won't be able to avoid. But I can offer you something that will ease the deep, deep heartache."

Even as my jaw clenched, I assumed she was just bullshitting me for more money. She would fill our heads with worry, then at the last minute offer a solution that would cost a buck. But the joke was on her. I had no more money to give.

Poor Maddie had gone white, her lips parted, her mouth slack. I put a hand firmly on her shoulder but she didn't respond.

The fortune teller wrapped the cards in a colorful handkerchief and set them next to her on the cart. She then opened the trunk and pulled out a large mason jar. She handled it as if it was light, but it was filled to the brim with a thick, black sludge that sloshed against the lid as she set it down.

"What is that?" Maddie asked.

I come out of the memory long enough to focus on the aquarium. It's easily ten times the size of that jar—oh, how times have changed. I grip the knife tighter and trace another red line down my ribs. It should hurt, but all I feel is the dripping warmth on my skin. How could I have forgotten that jar? The way the woman ignored Maddie as if she were already a ghost? The way her honeyed voice pulled me in as if I were just another one of her dupes in her sideshow ...

"What is it?" I echoed Maddie's words, but where her voice held disgust and fear, mine held interest. The sludge in the jar seemed to ripple of its own accord. I leaned closer, but the dim light coming from the tent flap didn't offer a good look.

"This is your future." She stroked the glass, long and slow, then tapped it with her painted nails. "Part of me pities you. You have no idea what's in store. And part of me envies you. For that very same reason."

"D, I don't like it," Maddie hissed in my ear. "You were right. Let's get out of here."

"Baby, we paid a dollar fifty. We might as well hear what she has to say." I patted Maddie's hand, but if I'm honest, at that point Maddie was gone to me. My entire world was that jar and the woman offering it.

The fortune teller unscrewed the lid of the jar, and the sound of wet tongues sucking teeth filled the tent. I leaned closer and saw that the substance was not true black but dark purple, like a bruise. A low pleasant hum came from the jar, but it sounded distant, as if coming from a faraway land.

"Please." Maddie's whine grated on my nerves in a way it had never before. She tugged my forearm, and I snapped out of the trance I had been falling into.

"Right. We should go."

The fortune teller gave a deep throaty laugh that was difficult to discern from a smoker's cough. "Afraid of your fate?"

I surprised myself by giving a short laugh, more confident than I have ever felt. "I think you have your connection to the spirit realm confused. I have no doubt you are looking for someone, and I pity him when you find him. But we're not who you think we are."

She stared at me, and for a moment I thought she would try convincing me again, but she only shrugged.

The feeling of weight in the air lifted as she placed the lid back on the jar, but she didn't screw it shut, and my heart kept pounding, as if that substance would leap out of the jar and lick me. "Of course. Let me make it up to you."

She moved the jar to her feet and opened the chest again, this time digging deeper. I kept my eyes on the lid of the jar, certain it would move any moment. The woman eventually pulled out a colorful scarf, similar to the one she had wrapped her cards in. She set it on the table and carefully exposed a gorgeous knife—a crescent bone handle and a dark blade tucked into it. The yellowing of the bone betrayed its age, and when she opened the blade, my heart leapt for it.

"How much?" I asked, even though my pockets were empty.

The woman ran one of her fingers over the flat of the blade, and in that instant I saw her not as a middle-aged church-going woman, but as she must appear on stage, clothed in loose and gaudy silks, a scarf over her graying hair, make-up rouging her cheeks to give her the hint of youth. "It's already yours."

What the woman said was true. In that moment, the blade was already mine, just as here and now it belongs to Emma. It has chosen a new owner, and I have only to surrender it to her. Then, I will be free of this curse. I can rest.

I sputter, and the blood rolling down my stomach chills and hardens on my skin. I wonder if the fortune teller felt like she was being freed, or if she was losing something. I close my eyes. There, in the very, very far distance, if I concentrate on with my whole being, I can hear the zhelani's hum.

I take the knife and draw it over my stomach, teasing

myself with how deep I can go. Pain oozes from me. It weeps like the blood running into my belly button.

In the fortune teller's tent, I had reached for the knife tentatively, not believing my luck. Sure enough, she waited until my fingertips felt the cool metal and then jerked it away.

"You just have to do one thing."

I knew it was a trap. Still, I asked, "What?"

Maddie squeezed my leg. A warning I had no intention of heeding. It was strange. I was not a hunting man. I had no collection of knives. My interest shouldn't have spiked so violently, but I felt a great need to own the object.

"You see, the knife is connected to the zhelani."

"The zhelani?" The word rolled like jelly over my tongue, and I knew she was talking about the liquid in the jar.

She set the knife down to pick up the jar and once again removed the lid. The scent of deep pine returned to the room. Maddie covered her nose, and I was afraid she might vomit. The woman paid no attention to Maddie, though. She took the knife and swirled it slowly in the sludge, releasing more pungent lower tones to the scent.

"The desire. Pure want, concentrated into a single being. One that wants. The zhelani."

"What does it want?"

The woman shrugged. "It's different for every person. Right now it wants me to give you this knife."

She drew the knife from the jar. It dripped with the thick black ooze.

"But I can't simply hand it to you. It needs to belong to you, and for that, it requires a sacrifice."

"A sacrifice?" I asked.

Maddie's nails dug into my thigh, leaving marks I would find the next day, but my focus was solely on the knife.

"It's a small sacrifice. Don't look so scared. A single drop of blood."

"You can't—"

"Fine." I cut Maddie off and held out my hand. "I'll do it."

The fortune teller, looking younger and younger the more I stared at her, held my wrist. Her grasp was tight, but her hands were young and supple, and a brief image of her painted nails running over my naked flesh flashed in my mind. She took the knife and pricked me with the tip just enough to make a fat, red drop swell against the metal. She smeared the flat of the knife against my skin, mixing the sludge with my blood, then tapped the knife on the lip of the jar, spraying droplets of the liquid into the glass.

"There." She set the open knife on the table. "It's happy now. Can you feel it?"

I couldn't feel it. I've learned since then that the zhelani cannot be happy. It can desire, and it can be satisfied. The moments of satisfaction are rare and definitely not caused by a single drop of blood. But back then I knew nothing of blood magic. All I knew was I had the knife and the fortune teller let us go.

I still have it now, and I can call the zhelani to me.

Come.

My body shakes, as if the zhelani is commanding and I'm obeying.

Come.

I spasm and fall. The knife clatters beside me.

CHAPTER FOURTEEN

I settle into the buzz of the creature. What did D call it? The zhelani. The word rolls off my tongue. It vibrates me from the inside, and though it takes a couple of days, I manage to not feel ill every time its voices rise within my chest. I relax and let my molecules spread. All that yoga. The breathing. The meditation that never worked. It was pointless. This is what I needed all along. This black ooze that opens me like the night sky. This is transcendence.

I keep waiting for the comedown. The stabilization. The moment when my fucked up brain takes control and I go numb again. But it doesn't arrive. Instead, the sensation of pleasure grows. At first it tickles, like a fizzy drink. Then it warms until it burns my toes. I scrunch my feet and bite my lip. It's been years since I experienced euphoria and even then it was chemically induced—a night of drugs, a week of medication. I don't pretend to understand what's going on, but I know it's that substance D injected into me that is giving me this bliss. And I want more.

Work holds no interest. Spreadsheets wiggle and bleed beneath my gaze, and on the third day I don't even bother showing up. There's a distant ringing—more solid than the one inside me—and I guess it's probably my boss. Maybe even Monica checking up on me. But I don't pick up.

There's no way I'm going back to that muffled cubicle and meaningless conversations with Monica. Not when I have this.

I lie on my living room floor, my head on a balled-up sweater that just happened to be near me, and I feel the creature turning inside me. I begin to turn with it. As we become one, its desire for pain grows, and it's familiar. I've wanted pain, too. I've wanted sharp, quick licks that drive me to oblivion. I've wanted blades and blood. My stomach undulates and my hips grind. Its need is deeper than the lake I used to swim in as a kid. It goes to the core, not of the Earth, not of me ... the core of something else.

A moan escapes my throat and I vibrate with the creature, but just before I fall off that edge into bliss, it tapers off.

I'm back in my apartment. The world disappointingly clear around me. My living room is messy, but normal. Average. Boring. I close my eyes, but when I open them everything is just the same.

I can't tell if the creature is teasing me. I can't tell if there's joy or malice in its give and take. Just expansion and closing. I let out an exasperated groan, roll on my side, and sit up.

Time has ceased to matter, but it's dark outside, so it must be either late night or early morning. Upright, I'm suddenly antsy. I'm not sure if the surge of the energy is mine or coming from someplace deeper. I'm also not sure that it matters.

Damn HR, pulling me down. Damn Monica. Damn whoever and everyone.

It's not just the call, though. The creature is retracting within me. Its vibration slows. Eventually, the discordant voices that made me shudder with ecstasy go quiet.

I thought it would be a relief to no longer hear the hum that was somehow deep inside of me and far away at the same time. But now that it's gone, I feel hollow, as if I'm missing the very essence of my existence. Most of all, I feel lonely. I pinch my forearm as if to say, "hey, you still here," but all I get in return is a small red spot that eventually turns into a bruise. The purpling is sweet, and when I dig my thumb into the small circle the ache makes me feel alive, but I'm still alone.

Years of solitude crash into me and my throat grows hot. My eyes fill with tears. I am so very tired of being alone.

"Please," I whisper. "Stay with me."

The night or morning or whatever earthly time passes irritatingly slow, and I wait for some kind of buzz—an answer—but the creature has abandoned me. The loneliness hits tenfold now that I've felt what real companionship can be. I pinch and pace and hit a wall just so I can feel some sort of vibration beneath my skin. But it's not the same.

Like a new mother with a crying baby, I go through the checklist: wet, dirty, cold, tired, hungry. Of course it's hungry. The way it slathered for people in the office. It wants pain. More, more, more.

As if in response, the creature bubbles in me, giving me the slightest taste of euphoria. Then it goes quiet again.

I slam my open palm against the wall, hitting it so hard my entire forearm tingles.

No response. It's learned that trick.

It wants pain and suffering? I can do that. I start up my laptop and connect through my tor client. There are a few gatherings happening in the city this week. Sex parties, a bondage workshop. Then luck. Tonight there's an S&M party in the warehouse district, not far from the West Tunnel.

I don't dress up. It's been a few years since I've worn latex or leather. Other women my size dress for the occasion, but I guess they must be wearing custom pieces. Everything I've found online ends at L, and once you get past M, the curves never seem to sit right. It doesn't matter though. I've been to enough of these events to know that naked is just as sexy as adorned in leather, and sometimes more appealing.

I don't recognize the man working the door. He's young and bright eyed, obviously subby and probably new to the scene. He wears jeans and a t-shirt, but it's not the clothes that give him away. It's the way he keeps averting his eyes as he asks for the password. An experienced sub would have more pride in the task their Master set them to. I give him the password, and he opens the door wider so I can see a couple of women taking money. One wears a rope harness, her breasts purpling from the pressure of it. The other wears a latex mask over her face, zipped and locked in back. I pay them fifty dollars.

"We've got an oral agreement for the rules tonight," latex mask says in a calculated chipper voice. "Have you been to this kind of play party before?"

"Yeah," I say, "a few times."

"Great. Blood play is only allowed on the splatter pad. You'll need to sign up before hand, and all pads require disinfectant after each scene. We use and respect safe words. You can watch all you like, but no joining a scene unless invited."

"Okay," I say. "That all?"

I'm aching to get into the main room.

"Enjoy," harness lady says, pointing to a curtain behind her.

The warehouse is cold, but the people wandering the room are in various states of undress. It's a bigger party than I expected, with maybe fifty people wandering around and one scene already going, with a man wielding a single-tail on the body of a thin woman who hisses with every strike.

"Emma." A short, balding man opens his arms, offering a hug. "I haven't seen you in awhile."

"Been busy, Saul," I mumble. I accept the hug even though Saul smells of sour musk and leftover sex. His pudgy fingers have probably been in most of the pussies in the room, if not tonight, then sometime. Never an organizer, he's still a feature at most of these parties, facilitating scenes behind the scenes.

"Sure, sure," he says. "You just watching, or looking to scene? Frank's looking for a partner if you're interested."

My pussy pulses. Frank is amazing with the floggers, coaxing his partners from orgasm to orgasm. He tends to seek out more pleasure than pain, and his aftercare is tender and sweet. Getting a spot with him can be difficult, and I've only been with him once.

"Actually, I'm looking to top," I say.

"You?" Saul doesn't bother hiding his surprise, and I don't blame him. The words feel wrong coming out of my mouth. I've spent the past two years seeking harder and harder tops. Someone who would drive me into myself—past the numb parts to the tiny sliver of emotion still alive in my heart. Finding a top that matched my desire wasn't easy, but it was clear I was a good submissive. Submissive and nothing more. When all will to live has left it becomes easy to accept and difficult to give.

But now, I have something to give. And something to take.

"I'm not sure anyone here is up for a new Dom. There are a few newer subs, but they're mostly collared and negotiating play may be tricky. Everyone else is more experienced, and people want someone that matches their level. You know how it is."

I do know how it is. Most of us crave the best. Not some clumsy newbie who can't even dip us into subspace. If we can't reach the ecstasy of that deep trance, why bother doing a scene at all?

"That's okay," I say. "I'm confident I'll find what I'm looking for."

Saul steps back, and takes me in. I hold my shoulders back and meet his gaze until he breaks into a smile. "I like the new vibe. What do you say we do a partner scene? I've got Rebecca lined up in an hour. I can talk to her about adding you in."

My stomach twists. The creature inside me doesn't want to share. But it's the best we'll get tonight, and I know it.

"Sure, that sounds good."

"Well, I'll be here," Saul says. "Meet me and Rebecca fifteen minutes before ten and we can discuss."

I spend the next hour wandering the large play space. They've put up curtains and dividers, trying to make the open space seem more cozy and intimate, but there's no hiding the raw industry of the warehouse. It's a place where things are built or stored. It's not a place for humans. The creature likes that we're out of place here, as if we're lined up for it to consume.

Patience, I whisper to it as I stop in front of a Saint Andrew's cross. A man is spread tight across it, his arms probably aching from being held up, and his wrists starting to burn from holding the weight of them. Behind him, a man wields a fat flogger, hitting the sub's buttocks without rhythm. The sub tenses when the next strike should fall, but there's nothing there. I can almost taste his humiliation. The shame mixes with the pain, creating an intoxicating cocktail that drives the creature in me to frothing.

In the distance, the voices take up their drone again. It swells in my chest, and the splitting headache I've been carrying eases. I stay and watch the light torture, and the creature slurps the thick emotion of the scene.

Of course it's not enough. Nothing is enough. It wants more.

Patience, I whisper again.

Then, it's time for my scene.

Rebecca is a head taller than me. She's heavy, but without curves. Her butt and thighs weigh down her body, and her small, bare breasts and narrow shoulders almost seem like they're floating. Her honey blonde hair hangs loose around her shoulders. I give her a quick hug in greeting and get a whiff of strawberries and cinnamon. The mix is overpowering and doesn't quit work. I'll have to find a delicate way to let her know to lay off the scents next time.

Saul hands her a hair tie. "Hair up, sweetie."

His words sound more like a suggestion than a command. It's the tone of a man who is used to being listened to. Rebecca obeys him, putting her hair in a high ponytail and then pulling it through the elastic again to make a sloppy bun.

Her cheeks are red with acne, and her shoulders echo scars of teenage picking. She wears a thong and black bra. Around her neck is a thin submissive collar with a ring and a small, heart-shaped padlock. It's more decorative than useful.

"Can she take the collar off?" The words are out of my mouth before I know what's happening, and I feel myself turning tomato-red at the suggestion. I know better than to ask something so bold, especially on a first scene.

Rebecca's mouth hangs slack. "Um, I ..."

Saul strokes her bare thigh. "It's okay, you can keep it on. Rebecca is a full-time sub now. Isn't that right?"

Her eyes light up and she nods.

"We are grateful Missy is letting us use you," he continues to croon, "and we promise to take good care of you."

Relief floods her flushed face even as disappointment tightens my chest. Saul continues the conversation, and I should be taking mental notes, but I'm not even paying attention as he goes over expectations and possibilities, she states her boundaries, and they negotiate the scene. At least Missy isn't here, negotiating for her sub. The scene's already watered down by Saul's presence and the collar.

Finally, the details are worked out and we move to a padded spanking bench shaped like a sawhorse, with planks for her to rest her knees on.

"Up," Saul commands in a low voice, just loud enough for me and Rebecca to hear. We don't have a crowd yet. Most people are divided between scenes already in progress. But Saul does a good job of creating intimacy from the beginning. I take note of the technique as I do up the cuffs on her wrists and calves.

"See how she can still move?" Saul strokes Rebecca's back. "We want her to feel absolutely cozy in her position which, for most subs, means completely immobile. Though, there are some who like the struggle. What about you, Rebecca? Do you want to fight the pleasure or submit?"

"Submit, Sir," comes her response. She doesn't even bother lifting her head from the sawhorse to face us, and I recognize that she's already going into subspace. A twinge of jealousy sparks in my chest.

Saul hands me a bag filled with lengths of rope. "You've tied before, yes?"

I shake my head. I suddenly feel completely unprepared, standing in jeans and a long-sleeved shirt like some kind of norm who has never seen a play scene before, let alone participated in one.

"Okay," Saul sighs. "Let me show you from the beginning. He takes out a length of rope and undoes the tie in the middle, keeping the bite in place. He maneuvers to Rebecca's hand, wraps the rope several times around her and the front leg of the bench, creating a neat column, then ties off, leaving a quick-release knot. He shows me how her arm, once free to strain against the cuffs, can no longer move more than a centimeter.

"Your turn," he says, getting out another length of rope and moving to Rebecca's other side.

My column is sloppier than Saul's, and Rebecca can move her right arm a few inches. But it's still better than just the cuff. I take my time doing each of her thighs, feeling Saul's judgement burn on my back. I've scened plenty of times, but always on the receiving end. I never had to give, just let pieces of myself be taken. When I decided to come here, I was thinking of how it felt to be beaten until the pain turned to pleasure. I wasn't thinking of how difficult it can be to give that sensation to someone else. Or something else.

When Rebecca is tied, Saul thwacks her bottom with his open palm. Her fat jiggles, and she tenses. But the ropes keep her in place.

"Good enough," Saul says. "We're going to warm her up barehanded. I want you to smack her bottom twenty times, ten on each cheek. She should get tense, but not fully frozen. And we're looking for red, not bruising."

I swallow thick spit collecting in my throat and nod. The creature spins in me, swirling to life, as if it's curious about what's about to happen, and I'm not sure if it's licking at my excitement or Rebecca's anticipation. I rub my hand up her thigh and to her bare butt. Her skin is soft and a bit cool to the touch. I have every intention of warming it.

I smack once, but the sound is low and dull. Nothing like the satisfying thwack I expected. I try again, harder.

"Cup your hand, fingers together," Saul instructs from over my shoulder. His orders are whispered; no one beyond me can hear, but I still flush.

This time there's a bit of the echo I'm looking for, and Rebecca gives a short, happy moan.

"Further down, you have to find where her curve fits the curve of your hand. It's different for everyone. Most tops can find it by the third strike, though."

It takes me five thwacks on Rebecca's bottom, her fat jiggling in random waves, before I find the position Saul describes, but when I do, she lets out a satisfied sigh that sends a ripple of unbridled joy through my body. The creature inside of me is not satisfied, though. The moment of connection is too short. It's a strike on my end, and then I am removing my hand, pulling back for the next swing, and her skin is too far away.

I try again, leaving my hand where I strike, feeling the warmth spread through her butt. The creature likes that. I can feel one of its ecstatic rolls rising in me, nearing the surface but not quite breaking. It likes this game—the complete surrender of its victim, her clenching buttocks in response to my firm pressure.

This time I thwack, then jiggle her ass slowly, echoing the rhythm of the creature within me.

It is expanding, and that expansion feels cold and crystalline. I take a deep breath. My chest is opening, my hands and forearms tingling. It is exquisite.

Again.

Rebecca's moan is low and throaty, as if she's chanting a mantra echoed by the beast within me.

I strike again, letting my fingertips brush down the wet strip of her panties as I remove my hand and wind up again.

Her moans aren't enough. I want to hear her scream.

I pull my hand back and release it with a snap, as if the creature inside me has created a spring. Again. Again. Again.

Her moan goes higher with each strike. No longer a moan, it's a scream.

And beneath the pleasure is her pain—not just the pain of the moment, although that is ripe and sweet—but the pain of a lifetime. The creature dances between me and Rebecca. It licks her oldest wounds, bringing up memories of childhood. Toddlerhood. She's wailing like an infant.

My own heart goes back to those days, too. I am alone, and no one is coming. I am alone and cold. I am alone and wet.

I am alone.

Separated from my mother.

The entire cosmic universe surrounds me, and I am vibrating crystals, threatening to break.

I am so close to shattering. So ...

... close ...

to ...

Strong hands pin my biceps to my side. I thrash against them, but they hold tight and pull me away from Rebecca. Through the push of flesh and leather, I get a glimpse of her ass. Long strips of flesh have been torn away, leaving deep red rivets of blood that flow down her shaking thighs as Saul and another man undo the ropes. Rough hands push me through a silent crowd. Eyes stare at me. Whispers collapse around me.

Finally, we're in the entrance-way, and the person propelling me stops.

"You should go," Frank says.

I'm glad it's him and not someone else. "What happened?"

"What happened?" he frowns, his usually gentle eyes stormy with barely contained rage. "You almost beat that girl to a pulp."

I move my fingernails over the pads of my thumb, pulling skin out from beneath them. "She ... she wanted it."

His eyes go wide and his teeth clench at the too-often passed around phrase. "Didn't you hear her giving her safe word?"

I shake my head. The whole room had been roaring in my

ears. No words could make it through. I can't explain that to Frank, though.

"You need to leave, Emma," Frank reiterates. "And don't come back. You're not welcome here anymore."

He shoves me towards the door, and I stumble into the cold night air.

CHAPTER FIFTEEN

I lie on the worn wood floor and remember things I've wanted to remember for many years, and things I don't want to remember now. Or ever. Memory is funny. It tickles at the edge of our mind, tempting us to different times, and when we give in and travel back to those days, they are dustier and dimmer than we thought they were.

I breathe slow and deep. My chest aches, the open wounds yelling at me to wash and cover them. But I can't get up. Not when I can see Maddie in her knee-length checkered dress with a small belt above the barely showing bump. Even with her makeup smeared from the sweltering evening, she looked fantastic.

"I wish you wouldn't have taken the knife," she said as we walked towards the car. "It gives me a bad feeling."

I sighed and wrapped my free arm around her shoulders. We walked a few steps connected like that, but we swayed and nearly stumbled, so I released her. Everything was more awkward now that she was pregnant. I had to be careful, not hurt the baby.

"You couldn't expect me to pass it up when she was offering it for free. If you don't like it, I'll sell it. Bet it will fetch a nice price."

"Oh, D, we don't need the money. Not so bad that we have to take something ..." She let her voice drift off, then whispered, "evil."

I let out a boisterous laugh and hugged her from the side. "It's not good or evil. It's just a knife."

Aches and pains filled Maddie's monologue as we walked through the dusty parking lot. It was dark, but the carnival was still alive behind us. Barkers called for attention and rides creaked as they swung and spun. I would've liked to still be there. But leaving early was something we would have to get used to for the next few months, maybe for the next few years, until the baby was old enough to come to the carnival with us. I tuned out Maddie's complaints and let my mind play with the idea of taking a son on the Ferris wheel. Or maybe it would be a daughter and I'd buy her spun sugar and watch her cheeks go sticky-red as she ate it. My chest swelled at that image, and I stopped Maddie to kiss her.

When we finally reached the car, the moon was high and yellow, turning the fields bright as dawn.

But it's not dawn here, where I writhe on my floor, splitting the closing wounds open again. I concentrate on the pain. Force it to keep me in the present. I don't want to go back to that night and relive that moment. But it keeps taking me there. Every time I get to the end and then I can't stop my hand—I cut myself again, and it loops through, telling me the things I've done. The things the zhelani has protected me from.

All I want is the zhelani and the anesthetic it supplies my brain. I want the comfort of ecstasy and its constant desire. *More. More. More.* For a hundred years I was so hungry that I couldn't remember what I did. But now the zhelani has left me, taking away its demands, and I'm alone with my memories.

"Let's take the back road home," I suggested. "Get some air."

"Sure." Maddie gave a resigned sigh that felt too common those days. She got in the car but didn't scoot across the bench seat to the middle where she usually sat. I couldn't tell if she was just exhausted or still upset about the knife. Probably a little of both.

I went around to the other side, opened my door, and swung myself into the car with such force that the springs on the seat sunk and rose. I wanted to put my hand on her knee, but she was too far away with her temple resting on the window. The car bumped along, and her head bounced with it. I slowed so the motion wouldn't disturb her. I had a feeling she wouldn't chide me for my caution this time. When her breath came steady, I assumed she'd fallen asleep. She slept a lot these days—always in the bedroom for a lie down. Mother said it was normal in the early days, but I couldn't help but worry about her and the precious life she carried.

Even though she fell asleep, I still turned off on the county lane that circled town and rolled down my window so I could smell the wet green of the fields. The knife, wrapped in its bright cloth, separated me from my wife. I rested my hand on its delicate bulk as if it were Maddie's bare knee. It felt warm. Alive.

Maddie gave a little jerk in her sleep and a sweet, indiscernible murmur came from her parted lips.

I laughed, quietly amused. She was always talking in her sleep.

Don't reach for her. The warning goes through my head

like a mantra, as if I can reach across time and space and save myself this century of heartache. I tell myself not to reach over to smooth her honey blonde hair. Don't take my eyes off the road. Don't lean to the side so far that ...

A flash of sleek brown reflected the headlights, momentarily blinding me. I jerked the steering wheel to avoid a phantom that had already bounded away, if it ever existed. The turn was too extreme, and then I overcorrected, and the car swerved, hitting the edges of its balance and threatening to turn over. A loud crunch, a slam, and then a thud that would eventually become a sickening sound. But right then I didn't know what it was. I was dizzy and everything hurt, and then it all changed.

I was floating in my skin like a bubble, protected from the pain I knew I must be feeling. My body moved, and I sloshed after its motion. It twisted until my eyes could see Maddie. So much red dripped onto her dress. She had gotten changed twice that afternoon. Didn't want to wear a dress that would pick up dirt, but all her favorites were white. Now the blood stained the shoulders.

Her shoulders.

Her hair.

All I wanted was to touch her hair.

Time must have passed, but I felt trapped in that moment, even as I reached for her.

"Maddie?" I'm not sure if I whispered or screamed. Something in me called to her. "Madeline!"

I shook her shoulder, but she was limp.

I run my hand over my chest, pressing tentatively into the open wounds. They aren't that deep. Probably will scar, but that's nothing new for me, and there's no serious damage done. Although usually the zhelani heals its wounds. I wonder how long it will take my own body to make scabs and scars. Will I begin to age now? Or will the remnants of that creature continue to heal me as the years float around me? Just a few weeks ago I thought this is no way to live—constantly numbed by the zhelani. But now things are coming into focus, and I realize that if my future is steeped in memory I don't want it.

Back in the car, Maddie gave a whimper-moan. My heart leapt like the wagging of a dog's tail. So naïve. So hopeful. I pulled back her hair with a trembling hand.

"Maddie? Sweetheart?"

"D?" It was more of a croak than my name.

"Shh. It's okay." I touched her shoulder, smearing my hand in blood. She was pressed forward on the dashboard, and her body went limp as I leaned her back against the seat. I pulled her close to me and let her bloody head rest on my chest.

That's the first time the desire rose in me. It was sweet and painful and undeniable. There's no way I could have resisted. Maddie's temple pulsed on my neck in a slow rhythm, almost like a lullaby.

I twisted and picked up the knife between us, still wrapped in the colorful scarf. As Maddie's pulse slowed, mine gained until it was racing.

I wanted to stop, but my hand maneuvered the tip of the knife from its handle, then to her breast bone. Lower, where her belly was soft and another heartbeat echoed mine.

"No!" I cried out, trying to move my hand away.

Maddie's eyes fluttered open, and I don't know if she saw or felt the blade at her stomach. Either way, she whispered, "D, I can't do this," as if she knew what I was offering.

No. Not me. It wasn't me.

I have twisted along the floor so long that I'm on the small carpet. I dig my skin into it, itching, as if I can dig these memories out of me, but they continue.

Once again I feel the way the knife slid into her so easily, like it was heated and she was butter. I jabbed up towards her lungs. At least there was that much reprieve. I didn't slit her down.

She gurgled a bit, soft and almost sweet, and then the light left her eyes.

"Maddie," I whispered. But she was gone.

CHAPTER SIXTEEN

It's been three, maybe four days since the play party. Time has completely stopped making sense. Some hours bright light filters through my curtains. Other hours I'm vaguely aware of darkness. Neither of them tempt me from what I can only think of as my lair. I've pulled all the blankets onto my bed and created a nest where I roll in a new stench that exudes from me. It's a putrid scent of decay, but I can't stop inhaling deeply, pulling the scent into my lungs and holding it there. It's like walking in the forest in early spring. Layers of decomposition smell earthly sweet and a spicy aroma of newness breaks through it all.

Work isn't even a question. For years it was something that gave me meaning. At least I was contributing. I wasn't worthless. But now I have found the thing in life that makes me unique. The creature is mine to hold. To carry. If that's not meaning, I'm not sure what is.

At some point Sally from HR calls to ask if there's been an emergency, and I'm stupid enough to pick up the phone in my incoherent state. She lobs soft balls at me, but I don't even swing. I grunt into the phone as if I've forgotten how to speak.

"If you're ill, we can work something out. An extended, unpaid leave is possible. But we need to know when we can expect you so we can handle your tasks in the meantime." Her voice is tentative, but beneath her sweetness, there's a trace of familiar boredom. She doesn't care if I return any more than I care whether a cell gets filled with a letter or a number.

"I won't be returning," I say, unsure where the words come from. It's like the play party again—my body is acting without me. My breath comes faster, and I sit up in bed.

She tells me to think about it. Take my time and get back to her. Everything she says comes back to time.

"Time has stopped," I mumble into the phone.

"Excuse me?" Sally's voice raises a pitch.

"I mean, I'm not coming back," I say more clearly. My heart is thundering, like it might burst from my chest. I hang up while she's explaining how difficult the job market is these days and that once they fill my position permanently there's no going back. What she doesn't realize is that I've long since crossed the line of no return.

I hang up on her, but keep the phone in my hand. I squint at the display, trying to make the icons take shape. The thought of contacting D flashes through my mind. This substance was in him. He would know what's going on. But then I remember the shell of him that remained when I left and I'm nauseated again. I can't bear to look at him. Instead, I open Tinder and start swiping.

No. No. No.

I'm not certain what I'm looking for, but I know neither the cute guy with glasses nor the skinny girl in the short black dress will do.

Left. Left. Right.

A couple of good ones.

I don't even see their faces as I swipe. Just shapes. A square person, one pear-shaped. An apple. A bit of a triangle. I like the one that's rounded and dimpled like an orange.

My messages ping. It's a guy I just liked. He's got a single picture from the neck down, wearing just white underwear, his hard cock straining beneath the fabric. His stomach is flat but not chiseled, and his forearm, though tense, isn't muscled. I realize what I was looking for. Someone weak. Someone I can overpower.

He says his name is Jimmy, which is probably a lie, as are all the other tidbits he drops in our conversation. I'm no better, though. I try to stay away from reality and the lies it makes us both spew. His banter is only so-so, and I would usually ghost him, but tonight I curl up on the couch and feed him morsels of desire.

Yes, I want his cock in me. Where? Does it matter? I want the ins and outs. Okay, I'll be specific. My throat. My pussy. My ass. Yes, I'm DTF.

Tonight.

Now.

We agree to meet at his place, which I realize is a bad idea when I'm already on the subway. D had taken all of his victims someplace remote. Someplace no one would hear us scream. And we *would* scream. As I'm on my way to Jimmy's apartment, I realize I want to make him scream. Then I want to silence him.

No. Those aren't my desires. I just need a good lay to get my head on straight. The murder bubbling in me comes from the black ooze, and once I satisfy my own cravings, I'll be able to handle its demands. Somehow.

His apartment is better than mine, as far as a crime scene goes, but the second I walk into it, I'll shed pieces of myself that can later be traced back to me. Too risky. I remember pieces of the play party—mostly arriving and getting thrown out—but the specifics are fuzzy. All I know is this time there won't be anyone to stop me.

I consider messaging Jimmy and asking him to meet me in the park near the subway station. It's big enough to have some shadowy spots, and he might believe I'm freaky enough to want to suck him off in public. Maybe I was a week ago, when I didn't care about living. But now I'm thinking about the wet grass seeping into my jeans and how grass stains are a pain in the ass to clean.

The subway hisses to a stop and as I disembark I realize I'm just one stop from D's place. I don't even have to go back through the turnstile. I could walk to his apartment and get some answers. But my skin is burning and I feel like I might burst. I don't have time for answers.

I pull out my phone and open the directions. Above ground, location services start working, and getting to my date's house is a matter of following a blue line as it curves along the map.

He lives in a low-rise apartment, nothing fancy. The hallways are low and wide, giving it a dormitory feel. I check his age on the app. Twenty-eight. I'm still considering his picture while I knock.

The person who opens the door doesn't look like his profile pic and there's a moment of panic in my chest. But the tightness settles to butterflies and then fades to assessment. He's at least mid-thirties, and that's being generous. Gray hair peppers his temples and he's got a firm paunch straining against his navy blue t-shirt. He's wearing light gray sweatpants, both convenient and a bit sloppy. His face has that kind, tired *dad* look, and I wonder if he's divorced or maybe still married and traveling on business.

"C'mon in," he says, stepping to the side and lowering his eyes.

He waits, and I try to decide what I want to do. If this was really about fucking, I'd most likely say nothing, turn away, and go to the club, where I could pick up someone a little more my style. But it's time that I'm honest with myself. The creature in me is churning with impatience, and this isn't about fucking.

I step inside.

"I know, my picture's a bit old," he says with a nervous laugh as he shuts the door. "I've never gotten around to updating it."

"Mmm," I muse.

"Do you want a drink or something?" he asks as I wander into his living room. It's lived-in. Not giving off an Airbnb vibe. So divorced.

"I don't drink," I say.

"I didn't mean ..." he stammers. "I have cola."

"I'm fine." I offer him a small smile. The poor guy's sweating around the collar. With what I'm about to do to him, I can spare a moment of kindness now.

And what am I about to do to him? This whole time I've been running on auto-pilot. The creature in me has numbed my brain, and honestly, I like it. I can be pleasure and action so long as it continues feeding me desire. I shake my head and swallow. In my mind I see the man lying naked on the couch. His bare chest has a smattering of dark red blood which slowly drips down towards the belly paunch and flaccid penis. "Let's go in your bedroom."

Relief and excitement redden his pale face as he nods enthusiastic agreement. "Yeah, sure."

But then we're in the room and there's that poignant moment of hesitation again, both of us waiting for the other to act. Finally, he launches at me and presses gummy lips against mine.

I instinctively press my lips into a seal, and he backs up.

"I'm sorry, I thought ..."

I roll my eyes and maneuver over to him. I put my hands on his chest, springy hair giving him a soft, teddy bear feel. His heart is thundering, and pity washes over me. Although, if he touched me, he'd feel the same thing. My stomach flips as I slide my hands around his waist and rest them on his butt, pulling him close enough to kiss. Slower this time, trying to see if something will build between us.

He gives a soft, high moan, and my stomach flips with desire. It rushes into my chest and my breath comes short. I press deeper into the kiss and the flame melts out, warming my shoulders. It creeps down my biceps to my forearms. My fingers curl into the softness of his pants.

I've never been one for foreplay. It feels too much like teasing, and like everything else in my life, pointless. I've always wanted the abyss of fucking—that moment when the brain stops chewing on a litany of sins and sits in silence. If it's hard enough and good enough, it's like running off a cliff, not sure if there's water beneath or just an void that you'll fall into and never come back from. I've always wanted the void, and now, I can have it.

My date has a hard time keeping up. He stumbles to the bed and fumbles with my clothes, but I'm in the moment and I'm willing to overlook his ineptitude as long as things keep progressing.

I peel off his shirt and help him wiggle out of his pants, and he's more attractive naked than I thought he would be. Even with his cock semi-hard, there's a vitality to him that was missing from my earlier vision. I wasn't wrong about the sprig of salt-and-pepper hair on his chest, though. I kiss down it, running the tip of my nose in its softness. My breath moistens the hairs and my lips press the wetness into his skin as if I'm imprinting myself on him. I kiss lower, nearing his belly button, and his cock begins to swell, jumping to thunk against my breasts and then sinking down again.

Pleasure rushes through me and I let out a low, throaty laugh. He coughs and echoes my laughter, his high and strained. This just makes me smile more, and I lick from his belly button to where his hair thickens, then run my chin down until my cheek makes contact with his cock. Now his moan is low, slightly desperate, and very real. It's the sound I've been waiting for, and this time I'm sure the flush of excitement running through my chest and hardening my nipples is all mine. It is too familiar to belong to the creature within me.

"I ... do you," he stammers again.

I roll my eyes and straddle him. I'm still on his belly, my weight pressing into his. "Do you want to be inside me?"

"Yes," he whispers, then clears his throat. "Yes."

I pin his shoulders and raise my hips. Inch by inch, I move down, until my swollen slit finds the end of his engorged cock. I swirl my hips, catching his hard tip; I ease it into me, letting myself slide down his shaft. The pleasure is immediate, both in my pussy and in his sigh.

I'm not quite on autopilot, but this is a familiar enough scene that I don't have to think about what I'm doing. I can relax my mind and enjoy myself. I don't have to double-check my work. I don't have to defend my choices. This is freedom. But tonight, something new encroaches on that moment of ecstatic release.

The creature pulses in my wrists, forcing my fingers to curl like kitten claws. I scratch hard down my date's chest.

The pain is unexpected.

Unwanted.

He hisses and squirms to get away, and I try to apologize, but my jaw is clamped shut. My fingers lash out again, leaving more welts on his chest.

"Hey, hey," he says with a quiver in his voice. "Can we slow it down?"

I want to agree. I beg my mouth to open and say yes. Instead, my throat lets out bubbling laughter and my hands rub over the welts, up his chest. My splayed fingers tighten and find the cylinder of his neck.

He's saying no, and I want to stop, but there's something in me saying yes. Yes. More. Please. It begs me to keep going. Tighter. Harder.

More.

The edges of my vision blur as if I'm the one being choked. I can no longer make out the lines of my date's body. His face is just faint shapes. My eyes close.

Yes.

I see him limp beneath me, his lips blue, his cheeks ashen.

No.

My eyes fly open and my hands break from his throat.

He's gasping. His cock has gone rock hard in me, but his eyes are filled with wet fear.

I scramble off him.

He's saying something, but I can't make out the words over a ringing. No heavenly choir this time, just a bleeding fuzz a bit too similar to the morning after a good night clubbing.

All I know is I have to get out of this apartment and away from this man.

———

The thing that frightens me most is that I didn't stop because I thought the man should live. I stopped because the method didn't feel right. His pulse beneath my bare skin was not how I wanted to kill him.

No. I didn't want to kill him at all. It was the monster

within me. It wanted to kill him, and now it's angry that I didn't follow through. I still feel it pulsing thickly through my veins, a slow sludge that barely circulates.

I stop in the park, fall to my knees, and vomit. I no longer care about grass stains on my jeans or what it may look like if someone passes me by. I need to get this thing out of me. But no matter how much I heave, only chunks of my lunch come up. The slick, black thing clings to me, refusing to let go.

At least I stopped. Maybe he'll have some bruises, but I didn't kill him.

I sit back on my heels and look around. The park is large and dark, the oak trees casting deep shadows on the damp grass. Across a field is a thankfully empty playground. Dim lamps light the jogging path. I stand and make my way back to it.

Up until now, answers were something in the back of my mind. They weren't nearly as important as the lush surrender to the pleasure of desire that coursed through my body. The zhelani gave me a moment of peace after a lifetime of struggle. I fucking deserve that. Don't I? But now there's no denying what that creature wants from me. It wants me to kill someone. If what I know about D means anything, it won't stop at one person. It wants me to become a murderer, and I think maybe it will get off on corrupting me as much as it enjoys the pain of its victims.

The night is crisp around me. Details are in sharp focus, as if I was in a fog that has lifted. I take my phone out of my purse and pull out a map. D's apartment is a twenty minute walk from the south exit. It will give me some time to collect my thoughts and figure out what I'm going to tell him. I quicken my step. What I will demand from him. Because this is his fault. We agreed he would kill me, not infect me with his fucking pet.

CHAPTER SEVENTEEN

I lean back on the couch, my naked legs sprawled on the carpet. My chest hurts like hell now, the open wounds burning. They're thin and shallow, nothing more than advanced paper cuts, but my head still spins from the pain. How many people have I inflicted this and worse on in the past one hundred years? I deserve this pain, and yet I whimper like a dog, begging it to subside as if there's still a god that would listen to me.

A century ago, when it was still only one person I had murdered, I walked back to the fairground, cutting across the rolling hills and sticking close to the line of trees that marked the nearby creek. No cars had passed since the accident, but that didn't mean no cars would go by, and when they saw the carnage I left behind, they'd start looking for me.

I swallowed, my throat burning as if I was shoving the knife down it. My hand holding the blade shook. I had left the bright scarf behind, but the dark metal came with me. Already, after only one kill, it was part of me—an extension to my hand.

My awareness was heightened. Every cricket chirping sounded like a symphony, and I could just make out the tiny splashes of water over stone in the creek a hundred yards away—sounds I had no right to hear. Not only were they beyond the bounds of my human hearing, I no longer had the right to hear God's pleasantries. I was a murderer. And—oh God, oh God.

I fell on my knees and wept. Then rose. The pain numbed just a bit, something in me promising it could take all the pain away. If only ... I just had to ...

The walk back to the carnival grounds was long. What we had covered in minutes in a car took long enough for the moon to rise over the hills and kiss the treetops on foot. When I got to the hollow where the carnival was tucked away, I saw the rides had been stopped. There were still a few lingering crowds, but nothing like the merry throng Maddie and I had waded through. I briefly wondered what time it was, but then realized things like time didn't pertain to me anymore. With one thrust, I had positioned myself out of life and its ordinary trappings.

Pressing in around this memory are a thousand other moments. Tramps through wet grass after a fresh kill taunt me. How many times did I allow the knife to drag through tender flesh and seek out the organs of my victims? How many times did I pull down instead of thrusting up, knowing they would writhe in pain longer if their lungs were intact? I cough, a gurgle coming up from *my* lungs. Something stinks of ammonia. I look down at my naked body and realize I'm wet with piss. I try to move, but the memories have me pinned to the spot. Through all of the groans and screams and noes, that single, worst memory presses through.

The carnival was a tangle of tents, and though I easily found the green, drab canvases that marked the carnie housing, I was hopeless looking for the fortune teller. I didn't even know her name, so I couldn't stop someone and ask for her. Still, how many fortune tellers would a carnival have? If I got the wrong one on the first go, I'd ask again. And again. Anything to find her and make this pain stop.

I was approaching a small group around a folding table lit with a few lanterns, long shadows looming, when a hand reached out and grabbed my wrist. The momentum of their grasp pulled me into the folds of a tent before I could protest.

"You're back." The fortune teller's hushed voice held a lilt of amusement. "I knew you wouldn't be able to resist."

"If you knew ..." I mumble.

She pulled me along a narrow path between tents, and I followed meekly.

"You smell of sweat and blood. Don't think I don't know what you've done, son."

I wanted to tell her I wasn't her son. I was no relation of hers or these carnival tricks. But my mouth hung slack, and I followed as sure enough as if I were her progeny.

A few twists, and we were back to her tent. Even though I had only been in it once, it felt familiar and, somehow, safe.

The olive green tarps drudge up memories of the war. Those were the easiest times to find willing victims. It wasn't until 1942, dug in next to a compatriot who had no idea I wanted to stick him as surely as I wanted to shoot those across from us, that I realized I could make my uncontrollable desires have helpful action. I could live by a code. I could control this beast as surely as it controlled me.

A ray of warmth spreads through my body. He thanked me before I slit his belly. He begged me before I took his breath. Hope that maybe I've been a good person despite everything, but no, the carnival wins again, and I'm back with the fortune teller.

She drew the flap shut behind us, and for a moment we were in complete darkness. I could smell her slightly sour aroma permeating the tent. Then she lit a gas lamp and set it on the table.

"You want answers?"

I scream at my past self to say yes. But I do what I originally did—shake my head dumbly from side to side.

"Listen anyway. There are some things you need to know, even if you don't want to. Things that will keep you from going insane. I know what I've done to you is cruel. But someday, you'll do it to someone else. You'll have had enough. You'll be tired. You will be merciless. Someday, you'll understand."

I nodded along. For fifty years I thought she was wrong. For fifty more I denied that she could be right. For the past ten, I've been denying I was like her. But now, the zhelani has left me, and I cry because deep down, it's what I wanted.

She pushed me back with one finger, and I plopped onto a narrow cot.

"One thing, know it has a name. The zhelani. Names are important, and sometimes the only power we have." She turned to the table. The jar still sat on it. She twisted the cap.

I come to my senses and scramble away from the piss, as if my movement in the here and now could force me to scramble off that cot and out of that tent. Somewhere, there's a knocking, and I can't tell if it's in the here-now or in my memories. The tent is so much more real than my apartment.

"Second. It's not from here. Not from this earth. Not from the same God that made you and me. Don't go bargaining with the devil, he can't help you. This creature is beyond that. It's beyond what we can fathom." She bent over the jar and gave a sound like gagging. It reminded me of Maddie in the mornings, and I finally stirred from the cot. But my head started swimming, so I didn't make it to fully standing.

The knocking becomes a pounding and I come out of my

stupor long enough to glance at the door. For a brief moment I think it's the police, finally found me and ready to give me my due justice.

"Third. The zhelani can feed in many ways. Desire comes in all forms. It likes death the best, but pain will do just as well. And in a pinch, pleasure."

The door of my apartment swings open, and I think I've found salvation. Something—someone—to distract me from what's next.

But no, I still see the way the woman turned from me, looking flush and round and somehow younger. She approached me slowly, a bemused smile on her full lips. She didn't bother with our clothes, only undid my pants and pulled them down to my thighs.

I hated myself in that moment because I knew I should feel guilt or grief. But the worst part was that I wanted it. I was erect with desire, not just a physical reaction to her chilled fingers wrapping around my cock, but actual desire.

"Yes," I moaned.

The woman echoed my moan with a hiss of her own. "Yes."

Then she pulled up her skirts and climbed on top of me, and I wanted her wetness wrapped around me. I wanted her to ride me. But even deeper, I wanted what she was ready to put inside of me.

Someone hits my cheek. More than a pat.

"D? D, wake up."

I pull myself from my reverie and squint at the face looking down at me. "Emma?"

CHAPTER EIGHTEEN

When I walk into D's apartment, he's sprawled out on the floor, completely naked, and covered in blood and what smells like concentrated urine. I cover my nose with my hand to keep from gagging, but the scent fills the room.

D's vision is caught in the middle distance and he's murmuring something about a tent. I call his name but he doesn't respond.

I consider leaving him there—going home and forgetting everything about tonight. I also debate calling for help, but I don't know who I would call. Neither of us wants the police involved. Besides, his wounds don't look too deep. So I cross the threshold uninvited and give him a few pats on the cheek, then a full-on smack.

That brings him out of whatever stupor he's lost himself in.

"You okay?" I ask as he scrambles to sit up, bending his legs to conceal his flaccid penis and crossing his arms over his torn-up chest.

"How'd you get in?"

I step back and assess him again. The wounds are barely

scratches. He'll be fine. "Door was unlocked. You'd think you'd check before you go off on a bender."

My words are harsh, but I'm not judging him. The strange urges I've been feeling, coupled with the days of euphoria, make me realize it's not always drugs, and I've always understood about not having a choice. After all, I didn't choose to be numb half my life.

"Let me rinse off and get dressed," he says. "Then we can talk."

He stumbles as he gets up, and I reach out to catch him, but he regains his balance. Part of me is afraid he'll escape out the window, but when I see him shuffle into the bathroom, I'm not so worried. That guy isn't going far.

She's in my apartment. Not Maddie. Not the fortune teller. Emma. She came back. Just like I returned to the fortune teller. Because once part of it is in you, the rest will call.

Lukewarm water sprinkles on my shoulders and runs in rivulets down my back and chest. It stings the wounds, and I dare not use soap or a washcloth, but I rinse off most of the blood and all of the piss and then grab a towel to pat myself dry. When I glance at the mirror, I see myself fractured. I barely remember hitting the glass. How long have I been rolling around in this stupor of memory. Hours or days? I take a step forward and trace one of the lines to the star in the center. My finger fills the small hole, and I pick off a sliver of silver.

With a deep sigh, I leave the mirror. I take my time picking out sweatpants and a loose shirt. Emma will wait. This is a conversation we both need. I remember the little information the carnival woman gave me. Three pieces of advice. Simple to remember despite the high I was on. When she gave me the entirety of the zhelani, I was completely out of my mind for weeks, if not months. I hid in the woods, slept in ditches, fucked women that would have me and killed men who wouldn't. When I finally came out of my frenzy, the woman was long gone, as were any answers I might get. This was a fate I never intended for Emma.

Mostly dry and fully clothed, I return to the living room to answer her questions.

———

"You came back," he says when he comes out of the bedroom in a t-shirt and sweats. I suddenly remember my date and what I almost did to him. I don't know how the memories, which should be fresh, were pressed out of me. But now that I find them, the piss on the floor and scratched-up chest are less intimidating. I am powerful. I can handle a scrawny thing like D.

I cross the floor and sink onto the couch. "I did."

"You want the knife."

I shake my head. "Yes."

The word shocks me. I frown and try again. "Yes."

Another shake of the head. "Yes."

He gives a slight chuckle and sits next to me. "It's got its claws in you."

This time I nod, my body and mouth agreeing. "It does."

"It came for the knife," he says. "You came for answers."

I nod again. "I ... almost ... tonight ..."

I can't get a full sentence out.

"You killed someone," he finishes for me.

"No," I explain. "But almost."

He shifts on the couch. Blood seeps through his shirt in small dark spots, and I'm overwhelmed with the urge to touch it. I reach my hand out, then pause.

"Go ahead," he says.

"You're not afraid that I'll ..." I still can't bring myself to say in.

"That you'll kill me? No." He takes my hand and guides it to his chest, wincing when my hand presses the fabric against him. "Look at me. I'm pathetic. The zhelani has no interest in people like me."

He's right. The creature had passed over the muscly men who would overpower me, but it also passed over the skinny guys who looked too weak to put up a fight. It wants a struggle, which D no longer can offer.

The pressure of her hand makes me feel alive. She moves it, just a centimeter, and the dull ache sharpens to a shooting pain that runs right to my lungs and heart. I lean back and pull her onto my chest. Our legs tangle on the couch.

She's stiff, not sure what she wants and what the zhelani is driving her to do. It's a sensation I'm familiar with.

"It's okay," I say. My natural voice is nasal and not as soothing as the booming voice that floats past my lips when the zhelani is in me. "We're just going to lie here and talk, okay? Nothing more."

She relaxes against me, letting more of her weight sink onto my thigh and stomach. But she's still ginger with my chest. The tiniest bits of the creature still clinging to my guts wants her to press harder. I want to swallow her. I want to take back what I've given her—what is rightfully mine.

I take a deep breath and try to still the desire rising in me. For the first time in over a century, I can control myself, and that ability is almost as intoxicating as the creature.

"Was this your plan all along?" she asks. "To put this thing in me?"

"First, it's called a zhelani. Names are important." I can almost hear the fortune teller speaking through me, laying out the future for this frightened woman. "But no, I didn't plan for this. I suppose I knew the zhelani was ready to move on, but I didn't pick you as its host, and I wasn't aware it had, either. I honestly thought I was going to kill you last week."

She draws a circle on my t-shirt, pressing harder and eliciting a wince. She doesn't apologize. "Zhelani. Why are names important?"

He's spouting some esoteric bullshit about gods and the devil and things beyond. I wouldn't believe any of it except I saw the rippling purple being living in his aquarium. I saw it go into him, and I feel it in me. At this point, does it serve anyone for me to hold onto the little bit of skepticism I have?

I want to protest. I want to rant and rave and pace the room. I want to be angry at him and this creature he put in me. The zhelani, as he calls it. But it won't let me do any of that. Over the past few days, it's gained more and more control over my actions, and tonight I've realized just what that means. At the moment, it wants to lay warm and cozy in D's arms. I let it. But it isn't me lying there. I won't give it that much.

"You went through this, too," I say.

He nods, and his eyes cloud over. They are definitely brown. I'm not sure how I ever mistook them for green. "I did. Over a hundred years ago."

He lets that sentence sink in. My mind reels in protest. He can't be over a hundred years old. Although, his skin sags now, forming wrinkles on his face and arms, and it has that papery delicacy that old people have. Lying next to him, I feel like I could be lying next to my grandfather. He even has that slightly medicinal and decaying scent of the elderly.

"Did you want it?"

———

Her question rattles me to my core, and for a moment I feel the last dregs of the zhelani retreating, giving me space to answer.

"The zhelani created a situation in which I couldn't not want it," I say, but that doesn't feel quite true. Even before Maddie died, there was a part of me that had been yearning for more. I didn't want to grow old. As much as we tried for a baby—a family—there was a part of me that had never wanted to settle. I breathe deep, feeling completely hollow and wishing I had just a taste of the zhelani's anesthetic now. "I suppose, yes, I wanted it."

She digs her finger into my chest and pain shoots down my spine. My legs tingle. I want to cover her hand with mine and make her stop, but I let her explore whatever this is. It is something I vaguely remember ... lying on the cot with the old fortune-teller's wrinkly body pressed close to mine. Whispers in the dark. It is a right of passage, and the zhelani demands it as surely as it demands its victims.

———

D's pain is intoxicating. The substance inside bursts from harmless little bubbles into jets of pleasure. A soft cry escapes my lips, and I run my finger deeper into one of his wounds. There are at least a dozen of them, hidden by his shirt, waiting for my index finger to find their edges and press.

Peel.

The thought comes like a command, and I'm so deep into subspace that I cannot deny what my Master wants.

"Let's take off your shirt," I croon.

D gives a sharp inhale, but he lets me remove the garment.

His white skin is filled with angry red marks. No scabs. Just weeping wounds, waiting to be explored.

———

"The knife made these?" Emma asks as she runs one of her cold fingers over a welt, separating the already healing wound, opening it to the sharpness of the air and dirty pleasure of her fingernail. "Where is it?"

I shudder as she presses a finger into me, going deeper now, getting the pad of her finger wet with first a clear fluid and then blood. So much blood over the years. "By the aquarium."

———

I don't want to leave him for the knife. This pleasure is too exquisite.

But there's a drone that sounds deep within me, and it commands. *Get the knife.*

———

My skin is cold without her next to me.

———

The knife is heavy. Solid.

Ready.

CHAPTER NINETEEN

Emma stands over me with the knife in her hand. Maybe it's a trick of the light or maybe my vision's blurry after our brief torture session, but the blade seems to be glowing. The usually darkened runes on the handle are lit golden, and the blade itself is a hot cream instead of its usual dark silver.

Memories stampede in my brain, pressing to the forefront, demanding to be recognized. But through the cacophony, one moment stands out like a zoo lion, unwilling to degrade himself with the press at the front gates. Its calmness draws me to it until the only thing I can remember is the fortune teller standing over me with the knife.

We had already had sex. That degrading part was over, thankfully. But this is something I hadn't remembered before. How had I forgotten the unnatural way the knife had gleamed?

The sex had shaken off the fortune teller's final vestiges of youth, and her skin hung limp and ragged from delicate bones that threatened to turn to dust with a single breath. She reminded me of my great grandmother wasting away in her bed on those final days—the ones when I'd hoped she would die so I wouldn't have to hug her again and feel the papery wetness of her sloughing skin on my cheek.

At that point I had already used the knife—God save my soul—but Emma still hasn't. She stands back a step, and I can almost see her shaking. I'm filled with the desire to pull her to me and tell her it will be okay, even though the lie would make me a hypocrite. She needs the comfort. She's a helpless little lamb, following the sway of destiny.

A sharp bile rises in my throat. I swallow it down and raise my hand. "Come here."

A little pride shoots through me. I can keep my voice from cracking, even knowing what's coming. At least there's that.

Emma takes a shaky step forward, and I recognize the jerky movement for what it is—that woman would have stayed planted there forever if she'd had her way. It's the zhelani coming towards me.

I take her hand in mine and draw her back down to the couch, the lengths of our sides touching.

"It's okay," I croon. "It'll be okay."

With one arm wrapped around her, I take her hand with the knife and guide the point to the arch of my ribcage.

CHAPTER TWENTY

The droning is constant now, rising in pitch, and I can barely hear D's steady voice beneath the bells. Each new strike sends me deeper into myself, and I can feel my innards twisting over themselves, a snake eating its own tail.

The point of the knife is pressed to D's naked skin, but the blade has no weight behind it. If he drops my hand, the knife will fall into his lap. Perhaps a less desirable position for some men.

Even without added pressure, the knife cuts a small dot into D's skin and slides into the groove of one of his earlier gashes. The blade twists, turning flat, and I grip it harder to avoid losing control. That little motion slides it in.

It moves like butter through his skin and sticks an inch into him.

His eyes go wide with shock or pain or both. But that damned ringing gets stronger, a gong being hit repeatedly, swelling in me until my spine moves in waves to the sound of it. Each breath crashes on the shore of that knife and the blade sinks deeper.

I give a gurgle of surprise. The next wave is rising and I

can't contain it. My body lurches forward, the knife slides into D, and my vision goes black.

———

The void is short. Just a few heartbeats and I'm through it to a purplish expanse. The place feels more vast than anything I've ever dreamed of. I am cold and wet. I try to look down, but my head won't move.

No, that's not quite right. I have no head. If I could look down, I'd see that I have no body. I'm just a mass of slithering ooze. A tingling sensation fills that space, and I'm growing, stretching out further. The pinpricks of pain get stronger as the needling stretches.

Something's wrong with time and space and self. I can't remember ... I can't ...

The pain comes in all at once. People passing gall stones and babies and, hell, just a shit when they have hemorrhoids —but the slicing, growing pain of it. The burning. There are knives and guns. So many bullets in stomachs and heads and faces. And how the skull feels when it's cracked. And why did I think of cracking because now there's bones sticking out of skin and shattering. Sickening sounds of car accidents and bike accidents and so many accidents. Some that were intended and the rending of bone and flesh that slips off it.

And words.

And screams.

And desire.

Unrequited.

And all the horrible things we do to each other.

And our selves.

It stretches on like that. Every twist of my self brings new horrors and more of that vibrating, needling gong.

When I extract myself from whatever hell the zhelani has taken me to, the first sensation I'm aware of is a hot wetness on my hands.

Vision returns in shades of gray at first, and a fuzzy outline of cheap, box-store furniture.

I'm straddling someone—the position is familiar enough these days. I don't want to look down.

My hands are hot. And slippery. And they hold something slimy and pulsing.

I retch, but don't let go.

CHAPTER TWENTY-ONE

Ba-bump.
Ba-bump.

CHAPTER TWENTY-TWO

Zhelani 28
5km away

About Me:

I'm looking for someone who likes pain. If you're just dabbling, swipe left. If you are ready to dive deep into worlds you've never dreamed of, swipe right. I'll fulfill your darkest, unspoken desire, but only if you beg me to. Let me hold your heart.

Interests:

BDSM, Knives, Breath-play.

ABOUT THE AUTHOR

Koji A. Dae is a queer, synesthetic writer passionate about mental health. A born drifter with plenty of dark stories, childbirth is the closest thing to eldritch she has experienced. After years of rambling, she finds herself strangely settled in the heart of Bulgaria with her partner, two kids, a cat, and a whole lot of responsibility. Working in tech by day, at night she writes about things people see from the corner of their hearts and all varieties of human relationships—with each other, with technology, and with the greater universe.

CONTENT WARNINGS

Hold My Heart contains scenes of:

Murder, violence, mutilation, and gore
Suicidal ideation
Self-harm (cutting)
Mental health issues (depression)
Sexual aphasia